"What do you think, Marcy? Can you picture Luke as a topflight reporter?"

"Personally, I think we'll be lucky if he just stays out of trouble long enough to finish the year as editor of the high-school newspaper."

"I think he's mellowing out," said Samantha. "He hasn't been in much trouble lately."

"That's only because school hasn't started yet."

"But now that he's got this burning interest in the newspaper, that could really make a difference," said Sam hopefully. "I think he's getting more serious. And he may be too busy to go around making waves. I hope so, because it's really important that we keep Luke out of trouble. Think about it, Marce. Since Happy is assistant editor, that means if Luke gets kicked out, she'll be moved right in to replace him."

"I don't *want* to think about it. I came over here to be cheered up, remember?"

Books by Janice Harrell

Puppy Love
Heavens to Bitsy
Secrets in the Garden
Killebrew's Daughter
Sugar 'n' Spice
Blue Skies and Lollipops
Birds of a Feather
With Love from Rome
Castles in Spain
A Risky Business
Starring Susy
They're Rioting in Room 32
Love and Pizza to Go
B.J. on Her Own
Masquerade
The Gang's All Here

JANICE HARRELL earned her M.A. and Ph.D.
from the University of Florida, and for a number
of years taught English on the college level. She is
the author of a number of books for teens, as well
as a mystery novel for adults. She lives in North
Carolina.

JANICE HARRELL

The Gang's All Here

Keepsake

FROM
CROSSWINDS

CROSSWINDS

New York • Toronto • Sydney
Auckland • Manila

First publication September 1988

ISBN 0-373-88032-4

RL 5.7, IL age 11 and up

Chapter One

"Stop the world!" a familiar voice wailed. "I want to get off!"

Sam looked up from her newspaper and saw Marcy standing at the foot of the steps, her dark bangs clinging to her forehead and her white shirt soaked with sweat.

"I thought you were at work," Sam said as Marcy mounted the porch steps. Sam kicked a little to make the porch swing go, in the faint hope of stirring a cooling breeze.

"I'm unemployed," said Marcy. "As of this moment Mr. D. is officially bankrupt. The kitchen equipment and the restaurant tables are about to go on the auction block. I knew the food was awful, Sam, but I didn't think it was going to come to this."

Marcy threw herself into the chair across from Sam, her lower lip trembling a little.

"Did you say 'bankrupt'?" Sam asked. "Does that mean totally blotto?"

Marcy nodded. "He didn't even pay us the last week's paycheck."

"But he's got to pay you for the time you've already worked!"

"Tell me about it! The money's just not there. No money. It's the story of my life. Now I'm going to have to go out and find some other job. I'd been counting on working part-time there right through the school year."

"But you'll get another job with no trouble," said Sam.

"Everything I touch turns crumbles," cried Marcy. "I can't keep a father, I can't keep a job. It's my rotten luck. Nothing's ever going to go right for me, Sam. Nothing. Ever."

It was true that Marcy's parents were divorced and that Marcy and her mother had, since that economic disaster, been living in a ratty little garage apartment. But all that had happened five years ago. Since then Marcy's luck had been no worse than anybody else's. Sam figured Marcy's sudden collapse in morale could be blamed on the heat. The thermometer on the porch read 102 degrees, which could take the fight out of anybody. What was needed was ice, not sweet reason.

"Hang on," said Sam. "I'll get you something cold to drink."

A few minutes later Sam got back from the kitchen with two glasses of lemonade. She put them down with a clunk in front of Marcy and watched the beads of moisture condensing on their sides in the heat. "Marcy, you know what you need?" she said. "What you need is something to lift you away from the disappointments of day-to-day existence. You need color and romance. And I've got just the thing, right here." She whisked the newspaper off the swing with a flourish. "Phillip Arrington Byron III. This new rich kid that's coming to town, the heir to the Byron tobacco fortune. I was just reading about it. He's the one for you. What you need is a rich boyfriend."

Marcy made a face.

"Lemonade not sweet enough?" Sam inquired anxiously.

"Look, Sam, I do not want to be one of your projects right now, okay? And I do not need a rich boyfriend. In fact, if I had a rich boyfriend I would probably scream in his face. Why do some people have to be rich? Talk about unfair."

"It wouldn't hurt you to be open-minded."

Marcy smiled, showing white teeth. "If you say 'rich boyfriend' again, I shall scream," she promised, her voice raising ominously.

"Don't scream! I won't do it again!" yelped a voice at the foot of the stairs.

"Luke!" Sam exclaimed, wheeling around to face the boy coming up the steps.

The summer sun on the boy's corn-silk hair gave almost a halo effect, but Sam knew him too well to be misled by it. Sam and Luke had been friends for a long time, and she was in no danger of mistaking him for an angel.

He charged up the stairs and grabbed Marcy's shoulders from behind.

"The gang's all here!" he said.

The three of them burst into song, Luke, slightly off key. He was directing the chorus of "Hail, Hail, the Gang's All Here," by waving a finger.

When they had finished the song, they slapped their right hands down on the arm of Marcy's chair, one over the other.

"I can't believe we're still doing this," said Marcy, looking at their layered hands incredulously. "It's going to look pretty silly when we're sixty-four."

"Let's be honest," said Luke. "It looks pretty silly now. It even looked pretty silly in the fourth grade."

"Not as silly as when we decided to be blood brothers," Sam reminded them, withdrawing her hand from the pile and leaning back once more in the swing. "Remember when Marcy cut my finger and I fainted?"

"You always were a sissy, Sam," said Luke.

"I don't know what I'd do without you guys," said Marcy. "You keep me from going absolutely gaga, no kidding."

"One for all, all for one," agreed Sam. "Friends for life. When you get to be rich and famous, Marce, I'll get to say I know you, and if Luke gets pitched into jail you and me can go halvsies on the bail."

"Hey!" protested Luke. "I want to be the rich-and-famous one. You two can be the ones in jail." He shot Marcy a curious look as he sat down in the bentwood chair next to hers and propped his feet up on the swing. Sam edged away from the sneakers. "Don't you ever wash those things?" she complained.

"Wash them! He ought to burn them," said Marcy.

Luke could have stood tidying up from head to toe. As long as Sam had known him, his clothes had behaved as if they were inhabited by poltergeists. Buttons popped off his shirts with abandon. He was the only boy she knew who could stand still in the middle of an empty room while his shirttails came untucked of their own accord. The seams of his pants tended to split to the point of indecency for no apparent reason—he certainly wasn't fat. And then there was his hair. She was sure that his mother made him comb it in the morning, but his locks seemed to be always in the wild disorder more often seen on Christmas-tree cherubs. The strange thing was that Luke had a way of making shredded clothes and uncombed hair seem like a new fashion. His basic good looks were unsinkable.

"The Board of Health will probably condemn your room next," said Marcy. "And look at the way you're sitting. It's a case for the Posture Police!"

"You couldn't be in a bad mood or anything, could you?" asked Luke.

"Marcy's summer job is kaput," Sam explained.

"So what? Summer's almost over. Who needs a summer job for just the last couple of weeks?"

"I am okay. I don't mind," said Marcy, desperately running her fingers through her hair. "So what if I can't afford to go to college? So what if I have to spend my whole life dishing out donuts at Krispy Creme?"

Too used to that lament to pay it much heed, Sam was already turning her attention to other things. She picked up her spiral-bound notebook. All the talk about summer being over had reminded her that it was not a moment too soon to make her list of resolutions for the new school year. Both Samantha and Marcy liked to make lists, but where Marcy's lists tended to be made up of sternly practical items such as "maintain ninety-seven average in algebra," or "save five hundred dollars by August," the items on Samantha's lists were harder to classify. A list she had made the previous spring had included reminders to "grow two inches!!!," "understand the motivation of Benedict Arnold (????)," and "be open to the poetry of life***."

Sam liked lists for their own sake. She liked their orderliness, their linear quality, the way they reduced her frothing thoughts to a format that made them look logical.

She sucked on her red felt marker a second and stared at the heading on the lined page, "Resolutions for the New School Year." After a moment she wrote, "l. Go steady with Phillip Arrington Byron III." She asterisked this item twice for emphasis. Just because Marcy wasn't willing to make use of this interesting new boy didn't mean that he had to go to waste. Samantha's own life could stand a little color and romance. Of course, if it turned out that the guy was awful, she could always cross him off the list. That was the nice thing about lists. They were not only logical, they were flexible.

"I don't know about you two," said Luke, "but I can't wait for school to start."

"Temporary insanity," said Marcy.

"If you'd just take the right attitude," said Luke, "school wouldn't get to you. You don't see me making myself crazy about it. Man, a hundred years from now who's going to care who aced Miss Richie's weekly quiz?"

Luke's grades continually hovered just above the level that would have required him to take the course over in summer school. He had C— down to a fine art.

"So do you know why I can't wait for school to start?" asked Luke.

"Jenny'll be getting back from Arizona?" hazarded Samantha.

"Jenny is history," said Luke. "Guess again."

"I think I've got it," said Marcy. "You've finally decided to bomb the lunchroom."

"Don't tease him, Marce. Okay, Luke, we know you get to be editor of the paper. I think it'll be great. We both think it'll be great, don't we, Marcy?"

"I get to tell you suckers what to do."

"That's okay," said Marcy.

"You're just saying that because you don't want to take orders from Happy," Luke said. "Tell me the truth, you guys, were you kind of surprised that Mr. Perkins picked me over her?"

"True ability will win out," said Marcy.

"Mr. Perkins knows you can really write," chimed in Samantha.

"I guess so," said Luke, his face turning a little pink. "You really think I can do it, you guys?"

"Sure," said Marcy.

"I've got big plans, some really serious ideas. We can do the same kind of stuff they do in, say, the *Washington Post* or the *Times*. We can set our sights high, really shake some things up. It's going to mean some changes."

"I'll say," said Sam, remembering the sort of material that had been the mainstay of the school newspaper since anybody could remember—school interviews, football coverage, updates on the grading system. It was a large leap from that sort of thing to the kind of writing that brings down governments and shakes Wall Street.

"We're behind you," said Marcy.

"Sure," said Sam. "We'll all back you up. Except—"

"Except for Happy, of course," supplied Marcy.

"I'm not worried about Happy," said Luke. "You really think I can do it, huh? Well, gotta go," he said gruffly, and he charged down the steps abruptly.

Sam and Marcy watched as the car with the license plate "Luke-1" careened around the corner and disappeared.

"I think he was getting all choked up there," said Marcy. "Who'd have guessed that old Luke cared that much about the newspaper? Did you hear him? Dreams of empire. Big ideas."

"Do you think he'll be able to pull it off?" asked Sam anxiously.

"I don't know. I can't quite imagine the *Traveler* turning into the *Washington Post*," said Marcy.

"It's a vision with him," said Sam. "You know, when I went in the video place to get *The Front Page*, the other day, I saw on the card that Luke had had it out eight times!"

"That's an obsession."

"I think he sees himself becoming some famous reporter. What do you think, Marcy? Can you picture Luke as a topflight reporter? Like Dan Rather, maybe?"

"Personally, I think we'll be lucky if he just stays out of trouble long enough to finish the year as editor of the *Traveler*."

"I think he's mellowing out," said Samantha. "He hasn't been in much trouble lately."

"That's only because school hasn't started yet."

"But now that he's got this burning interest in the newspaper, that could really make a difference," said Sam hopefully. "I think he's getting more serious. And he may be too busy to go around making waves. I hope so because it's really important that we keep Luke straight. Think about it, Marce. Since Happy is assistant editor, that means if Luke gets kicked out, she'll be moved right in to replace him."

"I don't *want* to think about it. I came over here to be cheered up, remember?"

"You know what she's going to be like if she gets to be editor. Bossy! Happy invented bossy. And she won't miss a chance to get her knife into you and me."

"I guess I'll just have to get used to covering the ball games in Outer Mongolia, then," said Marcy, her chin sinking dolefully down to rest on her hand.

"She's probably trying to figure out some way right this minute to get Luke dumped." Sam lowered her voice. "I didn't tell you this, but just before school let out I went back to the newspaper room looking for my pocketbook, and there she was, sort of breathing in Mr. Perkins's face and saying, 'Mr. Perkins, I'd do *anything* to be editor.' I'm not making this up, Marcy. His glasses were fogging over."

"She probably scared him to death," said Marcy. "I wouldn't be surprised if that's why he didn't make her editor. Isn't that funny? Up till now I'd figured it was just because Mr. P. was a male chauvinist pig and Luke was the ranking boy on the staff."

"But don't you think Luke will be a good editor, Marce?"

"I guess. Oh, sure, I do. Of course, I do," said Marcy loyally.

"He doesn't understand how sneaky Happy can be. All he's thinking about is getting the job done. He doesn't realize that she's going to trip him up every chance she gets and jump on every mistake he makes. And if he does go a little bit overboard, as you know he does have a tendency to do sometimes, or get in a little bit of trouble—"

"As he has a tendency to do sometimes," said Marcy.

"Well, nobody would be more pleased about it than Happy, is all I'm saying."

"All right, Sam, I don't like her, either, and I don't want her to get to be editor. But honestly, I don't see what we can do about it. It's kind of up to Luke."

"We can help! Just think of what it's going to mean to him if he gets kicked down from being editor. He's never cared about anything at school before. If this goes smash on him he might finally do something truly out-of-bounds. I'm telling you, this is important."

"I see that, Sam. I understand that. But what can we do?"

"We have to keep an eye on him. Support him during staff meetings and keep an eye on him outside of them."

"I guess you're right," said Marcy doubtfully. "We've got to do our best to keep old Luke in line," she said. In a low voice she added, "I just don't see how."

But Sam didn't seem to hear Marcy's softly voiced doubts. Sam sucked on her marker for a second, then added an item to her list—"Keep Luke out of trouble!!"

Chapter Two

When the rain finally let up the next afternoon, Sam drove over to Westridge Plaza to pick up her mother's allergy prescription. She was wearing short shorts not just because she knew she had good legs but also because shorts were the only clothes that made sense in the sticky heat that had settled over the town after the rainstorm. A shapeless felt hat that had once belonged to her grandfather was pushed down to her ears until it covered most of her straight blond hair.

As soon as she got out of the car, she saw a boy about her age standing in front of the ice-cream shop. She blinked at him for a moment from behind her rose-colored sunglasses, and after some reflection, decided she had never seen him before. She was sure she would have remembered him if she had.

Just then an old green Pontiac roared across the lot. It swerved slightly as it passed the boy, and for a breathless moment Sam was afraid she was going to be a witness to vehicular homicide, but the car merely hit the large puddle that stood in front of the boy and roared away, spewing mud onto the sidewalk. Sam watched aghast as the Pontiac made its getaway. The mud spattered on the car had not obscured its license plate, which clearly read Luke-1.

The boy on the sidewalk had jumped back at the car's approach but had not been able to avoid being slapped by the wave of mud. His white bucks were covered. The once-immaculate chinos were spattered all over, and he was wiping his hand across his eyes trying to get the mud off his face.

Sam ran over to him. "Here, take my handkerchief," she said breathlessly. "That driver—what a pig! Honestly, there ought to be a law."

"I think I saw his license plate," the boy muttered, pausing a second to spit some mud out of his mouth. "It looked like "uke" or "ike" something. God, I'd love to get my hands on him."

Sam was dismayed to note that the boy looked easily five inches taller than Luke.

"Probably it said 'no-nuke,'" said Sam quickly. "Antinuclear feeling is pretty strong around here. You could wash up some inside the ice-cream shop. They have a bathroom. I'll show you."

Sam led him inside to the bathroom. While he washed up, she ordered two ice-cream sodas, hoping that ice cream would help with the burning anxiety that seemed to have settled in the pit of her stomach.

She had never understood what demon possessed Luke. Maybe in this case he couldn't resist such a deliciously inviting puddle. His sense of mischief was never far below the surface.

She heard the door to the bathroom open behind her and bounded up out of her chair. "Here I am," she said brightly. "I hope you like chocolate. I got you a soda."

He came over to her table and sat down. He had not been able to remove all of the mud from his clothes, but once he was sitting down at the table he looked fairly presentable, though he showed some effects of his experience. His nose was pink where he had scrubbed the mud off of it, and his wet hair stuck out in odd spikes on top. The brown eyes looking at Sam were watering and bewildered. Having 20-20 vision herself, Sam did not recognize the befuddled look of the contact lens wearer who has had to take out his lenses. She only saw with a pang that this was a fellow mortal sorely in need of her help. Very possibly, she decided, he was not too bright.

"I hope you'll let me treat you to the ice cream," Sam said. "I don't want you to get a terrible impression of Fenterville because of what just happened."

"How did you guess I was new here?" the boy asked.

"I don't know," said Sam, wrinkling her nose. "I guess I thought I would have seen you around somewhere before if you'd been here very long. You know, like even if you don't actually know every kid in school, they look a little bit familiar, like your dental hygienist or the man at the dry cleaners or something. Did you just move here?''

The boy ran his fingers through his wet hair. ''Yeah. I'm supposed to be going to Lee this fall. Where do you go to school?''

''Lee. Well, it is the only school in the city, actually. I mean, unless you live out in the county, you have to go to Lee. What year are you?''

''Junior,'' he said.

''Me, too. Gee, isn't that a coincidence?''

''I guess I'm going to be kind of lost at first, until I find my way around.''

''I can give you some pointers,'' said Sam promptly, glad he was making it so easy for her to help him. ''You see, I've lived here my whole life, and I know how it works.''

''Is there some big mystery about it all?'' he asked, frowning at her.

''You have to find your niche, that's all,'' Sam said. ''You see, every school has its social setup, and you need to find your place in it.'' Sam noticed that he was staring at her legs, and she tucked them a little self-consciously under her chair. She fished out her spiral-bound notebook and her red marker. She would have to be very concrete with this boy, she decided. She would take things slowly and draw an illustration to be sure he was catching on. She opened the notebook and drew a triangle on the inside of its cover.

''See here?'' she said. ''These are the main divisions of the school. At the bottom here we'll write Brains. Like my best friend Marcy is a brain. That's her niche.'' Glancing up briefly at his confused eyes, she hurried on. Brains, she sensed at once, would not be his niche. "Now here we put Jocks," she said, printing the word at the apex of the triangle. She looked at him hopefully. "You don't happen to be good at sports, do you?"

"Tennis."

"You don't play basketball or football?"

He shook his head.

"Too bad, well, and the third major niche is here—Social." She printed the word at the third point of the triangle. "That takes in pretty much everybody else," she said.

"So where do you fit in?" He had pulled the notebook toward him and was bent over it, looking at it closely. She saw his eyes widen and realized he was reading her list of resolutions for the school year. "You're looking at the wrong side," she said kindly. She reached over and folded the resolutions page behind the cover where it would not confuse him. "The illustration I drew is here on the inside of the cover, you see. Jocks, Brains, Social. Where do I fit in? I guess I'd have to say 'Social.' You know, I like people, like to dance, I'm on the Student Council. Now within each of these major niches, of course, there are other groups. Like in the Brains bunch you've got the math-science-club bunch and the computer freaks as subgroups."

"You mean cliques?"

"Groups of friends, anyway." Sam's parents were always preaching against cliques, and she instinctively shied away from the word.

"I'm not exactly sure how I find my niche," he said.

"I'll help you. I think maybe you should go out for football. Or maybe basketball. Basketball is very big around here. If you play tennis, I don't see why you couldn't do one of the big team sports. They all have to do with coordination and hitting balls, after all." Sam was very vague about sports. Her own ambition in sports was limited to keeping a respectable distance between her and any moving ball, which was why she preferred soccer, where you actually had to chase the ball, to volleyball and baseball, where the thing had an unfriendly habit of popping out of nowhere to hit you.

He shook his head. "Basketball and football aren't my games, I'm afraid."

"Are you sure?" Nobody could understand an aversion to team sports better than Sam, but she recognized that this was rather more of a handicap in a boy than a girl.

"I'm sure."

"Too bad. That's the fastest way for a boy to get to be known around school. In a big school like Lee it helps if you do something that makes you stand out. Well, what about people? Do you like people?" she asked.

"Sure."

"Do you like dancing?"

"I guess I haven't done too much dancing."

"I'll teach you," said Sam impulsively. "You can come over to my house. Do you have a car?"

"I can get there," he said.

"Oh, I can pick you up. Where do you live?"

"Don't worry about it," he said. "I'll get there. What's your name?"

"Good grief, I haven't even introduced myself. I'm Sam Morrison. Let me write my address down for you here."

"I'm Pip," he said. "Pip, uh, Winston."

"Well, welcome to Fenterville, Pip," she said, beaming at him.

Wednesday, Samantha sat on the front porch waiting for Pip to come for his first dancing lesson. Her parents had so far ignored all her arguments for installing central air in their big old house, so Sam spent most of every summer on the front porch, drinking gallons of lemonade. Privately, she suspected her father of signing up to teach summer school just to get in air-conditioning. Fanning herself a little with her hat, she wished she could follow his lead.

She spotted Pip down the street, walking with long strides, glancing up now and then to check the house numbers. She could hardly believe Pip preferred walking in this heat to accepting a lift from her, but she chalked it up to a macho hang-up. Boys could be very weird about cars. They seemed to think not having one was some kind of disgrace.

She leaned over the banister and waved. "Hey!" she said. "Over here, Pip!"

He glanced in her direction and for a second looked blank, as if he had forgotten who she was. But then he broke into a smile of melting charm. Smiling like that, he was a surprisingly attractive boy. Long legs. Tan. Only a bit slow on the uptake, Sam noted. It was a lucky thing she was there to help him out.

"The stereo's in the living room," she explained when he got up to the porch. "Why don't I put on some music, and we can get started?" She congratulated herself on having had the foresight to tie Fruitcake, the family beagle, back by the garage. She sensed Pip was a little shy, and Fruity's insane baying wouldn't have helped put Pip at his ease. "We can dance right out here. There's plenty of room and we won't have to worry about breaking anything. Hang on. I'll run in and turn on the music."

Once inside she turned the stereo on loud and threw open the front window so the music could be heard out on the porch.

"The basic thing about dancing," she explained when she returned to Pip, "is just to listen to the beat and then let yourself move with it. Like this."

Pip leaned against the banister and watched her dance with obvious admiration.

"Come on," she urged. "You try it. Move with the beat." She whirled, narrowly missing one of the porch chairs.

"I wouldn't even know where to start," he said.

"Start by moving your arms. You can do that, can't you?" she said. She reached for his hands. "Like this," she said. "You do this, okay? Now come on, loosen up, move a little."

He pulled away from her. "I don't think dancing is my game either," he said. He looked amused, which annoyed Sam a little. After all, she was going out of her way to help him.

"I just feel so stupid," he explained.

"Everybody feels stupid when he's just learning," she said. "You have to try."

"If it's going to take dancing to find my niche, I guess I'm not going to fit in."

Sam plopped down in a chair, panting, and kicked her shoes off. "Okay, you're not a dancer. You can't be if you can listen to that beat and not move."

"We could try slow dancing," he suggested hesitantly. "I've done a little of that, but not lately. Maybe I ought to work on it."

"I'd have to change the record," said Sam. "Oh, well, all right. I'll go change it. Move the rest of the porch furniture over to the side while I'm gone, okay?"

There was something different about Pip today, but it was hard for Sam to put her finger on it. Yesterday he had seemed so sweet and confiding, the way he had let her lead him around and explain things to him. Of course, she reminded herself, if he was gaining self-confidence, that was certainly a good thing.

After she changed the record, she felt almost carried along by the slow melody coming from the stereo speakers. Sam had always liked to dance. One of the family snapshots of her taken when she was three showed her wearing earphones almost as big as her head and grooving to the music with a goofy little smile on her face.

When she came back out on the porch, Pip looked at her approvingly and drew her close to him until her nose was pressed hard against his shirt.

"I don't think people dance this close these days," Sam managed to say as she pulled away, rubbing her nose a little. Even though they were just dancing, she found it a little embarrassing to be squeezed up next to someone she had just met.

"Sam, you know that car yesterday? The one that did a number on me? I've been thinking—there can't be that many old green Pontiacs in a town this size."

"You'd be surprised," said Sam in a rush. "I have an old blue Plymouth my sister left when she went away to college. I mean, you'd think nobody else had a car as old as that, but every time I park it at the mall it seems like the parking lot is full of ancient blue Plymouths. Hundreds of them. Thousands. I'm even thinking about putting a daisy on the antennae. But anyway—" she swallowed "—why were you thinking about that car?"

"I'd just like to break that guy's neck for him, I guess," Pip said, holding her close again. "Last night I had to give my shoes a decent burial."

"Yo, Sam!" called Luke's voice from the foot of the stairs. "Tacos, keed! Let's go pig out."

Sam held on to Pip's arms. "It's just a friend of mine," she said hoarsely. She wondered if Luke's green Pontiac was parked right out front but she was afraid to turn around to look. She could hear footsteps thundering up the stairs. She wished Pip weren't so much bigger than Luke.

"Sam!" yelled Marcy. "Look!"

Sam unscrewed her eyes and turned around. There stood Marcy, bouncing excitedly on the balls of her feet and holding so many helium balloons that she seemed in danger of taking flight any minute. Luke, standing behind her, was smiling one of those incalculable smiles of his that could have meant anything. Sam was sure Luke recognized Pip as the guy he had splashed.

"Luke's cheering me up," Marcy said. "We've rented a bicycle built for two, and we thought we'd see if you wanted to get your bike and come along with us, but we didn't know you had company." Her eyes traveled the distance from Pip's sneakers to his dark hair.

"This is Pip Winston, Marcy, Luke," said Sam. "He just moved to town." She wondered what they would make of Pip. Sam scarcely knew what to make of him herself. She had only just noticed that when he held her close she had trouble breathing.

"Where you from, Winston?" asked Luke.

"Virginia. We only got here on Wednesday."

"You play basketball?" asked Luke.

"Nope."

"Football?"

Pip shook his head regretfully.

Sam wished Pip would turn on that smile of his. Marcy and Luke didn't seem to be exactly warming to him.

"Well, you guys want to go get some tacos or what?" asked Marcy.

"My bike's got a flat tire," said Sam. "I think the tube's busted."

"Too bad," said Marcy, looking at Pip. "I guess we'll catch you later."

"Sure, see you around, Winston," said Luke.

There was a brief pause after they had gone. Then Pip said, "So those are your friends."

"Yes, my best friends," said Sam. There was something odd about Pip's tone. For the first time Sam wondered if he had made the connection between Luke and the "uke" on the license plate. Fortunately she was able to comfort herself with the reminder that he was a bit slow.

Chapter Three

The bell that rang to begin school sounded like an electronic frog groaning about the end of summer. Smothering a yawn, Sam wondered why she had been so eager for school to start. She had forgotten that it began so indecently early in the morning. Ten minutes of eight was roughly an hour and fifty minutes before her mind normally woke up. She was finding it awfully hard to concentrate on what Marcy was telling her. "All I'm saying," Marcy went on, "is just be careful he doesn't hook onto you like a leech and not let go. I called you on Monday, and you and Pip were going to the library. I called you on Wednesday, and you and Pip were going swimming. Has it ever occurred to you he may just be using you because you have a car?"

"I like him."

Along with a mass of other kids they were moving past long lines of lockers toward their assigned homerooms.

"I remind you that it was you who told me he wasn't too bright."

"I may have been wrong about that."

"And what about your plan to enrich your life by going out with that rich kid?"

"I can still do that," Sam said, yawning, "if the guy ever shows up. The thing is, Marcy, Pip doesn't know anybody yet. Once he knows some more people it'll be different. Right now he needs me."

"Ha. That boy is about as helpless as a barracuda." Marcy turned into Mrs. Hughes's room, and Samantha went on down the hall to her own homeroom. She realized she hadn't been spending enough time with Marcy; that was why Marcy was acting so cross. It wasn't a good idea to take people for granted.

At lunchtime, when Sam took her tray outside to one of the picnic tables, she was careful to look around for Marcy. She had promised herself not to give Marcy and Luke any reason to feel neglected just because she happened to be spending some time with a boy. But while she was looking around for Marcy, she spotted Pip coming out of the covered walkway where the vending machines stood. He stood out for her as if he were outlined in red marker. She didn't know what it was about him that pulled her eyes toward him. It couldn't be looks. Sam knew better-looking boys than Pip. It was very strange. She couldn't remember ever being so aware of somebody.

Marcy appeared suddenly at her elbow. "Greetings," she said, dropping her tray onto the table beside Sam. "I've got Beasley for algebra. What have I done to deserve it? Was I a politician in my past existence? Will somebody please explain this to me?"

"What do you care?" Jack Merrick called from the other end of the table. "You always get an A anyway."

Toni Harmon pulled up a chair. "Anybody seen Lukey?" she said. "I don't seem to have him in any of my classes. I heard that he and Jenny are finished. Is it true?"

"I hate to disappoint you, Toni," said Marcy, buttering her bread, "but now that he and Jenny have split, he's decided to study for the priesthood."

"Very funny," said Toni. "Hey, did you hear about Ari Byron's grandson? You know, the new heir to Bright Leaf Tobacco? He took out six patents before he was fifteen and was identified as gifted and talented by the Duke Talent Search Committee. I hope this is not the guy who's going to set the curve in algebra."

"That's not what I heard," said Marcy. "I heard this Byron kid's not quite right in the head. The Byrons are already in town, this guy in my homeroom said, but nobody's seen him because the family likes to keep him out of sight. He's just taken out for short walks at midnight."

"Maybe he's one of those eccentric geniuses you're always hearing about," said Toni, tossing her sunbleached hair.

"Yeah, like Marcy," said Jack.

Marcy always ignored gibes about her grades, but Sam did not feel bound to take the same high-minded approach. "Would you lay off, Jack?" she said. "It's not Marcy's fault you flunked algebra, you know."

Pip materialized at their table. A shiny red apple from the vending machine wobbled on his tray as he sat down beside Sam.

"My records haven't got here yet, and my schedule is all fouled up," he told Sam. "I didn't even sign up for home ec but I'm scheduled for it first and second periods."

"Congratulations," said Marcy, "you'll make some woman a wonderful husband."

"It's the computer," said Sam. Pip's hand touched hers under the table, and she could feel herself smiling. It was not that she was falling for him, exactly, she told herself, but it was nice to have him around, nice to have him sitting at the lunch table, nice to watch him digging into those mashed potatoes.

"Count yourself lucky," Marcy told Pip. "Last year they had Mike Lambert scheduled for three consecutive periods of gym. By lunchtime he'd run the obstacle course so many times, they had to call the rescue squad to resuscitate him."

Sam licked her lips and tried to stop smiling. She was afraid she might have a very stupid expression on her face. "Make an appointment to see the counselor," she suggested. "They'll get it all straightened out. There's always a lot of confusion at first. That's why none of the teachers give much work the first week. Did you find your way around all right? You didn't have any trouble getting to your classes, did you?''

"Are you new?" asked Toni, interested. "Let me warn you—don't sit around the fountain. The fountain is for seniors only."

"So what are they going to do to me if I did sit around the fountain?" asked Pip.

"*Kill* you," said Toni. "Somebody ought to fill this boy in on the basics. Has anybody shown you the Wishing Tree yet?"

"I'll show him after lunch," said Sam. She did not like the way Toni seemed to be zeroing in on Pip. Toni Harmon was entirely too wild for a nice boy like Pip. The next thing you knew, Toni would be asking him to those parties of hers where the smoke smelled funny and there never seemed to be any parents around. Sam realized that she still felt responsible for Pip, even though he no longer wore that bewildered expression he had had the day she met him. Looking up, she saw Happy coming out of the cafeteria. Judging from her porcelain-pale complexion, she might have spent the entire summer underground with other low forms of life. Samantha had to face the fact that unless some unusually gorgeous boy lay in Happy's path, the chances were she was heading in their direction. She often ate with Marcy and Sam when no one more appealing was around. Of course, Sam reminded herself, she did want Pip to get to know some people, but not Toni, exactly, and certainly not Happy.

"I could show you the Wishing Tree now," said Sam, jumping up.

"I just started eating," protested Pip.

"Bring it with you," said Sam, snatching up his apple.

A minute later they were loping across the lawn past the gym.

"It's over here," said Sam. Just past the gym was a slope where excavations for a swimming pool had been begun and then abandoned when the city passed cost-cutting measures. A black pine clung to the edge of the slope, its low, twisted branches spread generously around it to make an impenetrable thicket. The pine had the usual tight green pine cones, but they were scarcely noticeable next to the fluttering bits of paper that had been attached to its branches, some with paper clips, some with safety pins or rubber bands. One or two papers were simply wedged in between the branches.

Most of the messages on the tree were plainly worded wishes for romantic or academic success, but there were plenty of more prosaic ones, such as "Firebird, 100,000 mi., very clean, $900 firm" and the ever-popular "Free kittens to good homes."

Pip read aloud, "'B in calculus—A.A.P.' The guy should try studying if he wants a B in calculus. You aren't going to tell me anybody believes in this."

Sam coughed a little. "That tree is the only thing that pulled me through second-year Latin."

"'M.J. to R.M.—All is forgiven. Call me,'" Pip read wonderingly. "It's weird. It's like some primitive tribal custom."

"Don't knock it before you've tried it," said Sam. "Doesn't this place have a nice feel to it? It's so quiet here and so full of wishes." She moved around the tree, reading the notices. "I'm keeping my eye out for a cheap desk," she explained. "When Robin left for college she took the only decent one in the house with her."

A boy and girl sat down at the edge of the slope on the other side of the tree and began unpacking their lunches from paper bags. After a while Sam and Pip sat down on the grass, too. It was a sunny day but the shadow of a cloud was moving across the grass. Absentmindedly, Sam took a bite of the apple.

"Hey!" protested Pip. "Cut it out. I'm starving."

"Sorry," said Sam. She put the apple down. Pip unwound the napkin he had wrapped around his makeshift meat-loaf sandwich and began to eat while Sam watched him. She loved to look at his eyes. They were just the color of iced tea, she decided.

"Nice place to eat lunch," he said. He carefully wiped his fingers with the napkin, then put his free arm around her. "We could eat lunch here tomorrow. I like it. Lots of privacy."

Sam regarded him a little anxiously.

"Pip, you've met my parents, haven't you?"

"Yup, nice people."

"And you've been to my house."

"Are you getting at something?"

"It's just that it seems to me, sometimes, that you might as well have dropped down out of the sky. Like in those sci-fi movies when they have a total eclipse of the sun and people from other planets show up disguised as human beings."

"Is that supposed to be some kind of compliment? I remind you of an alien?"

"I'm just saying that I can't imagine you fitting into any sort of background. Do you see what I mean?"

"No. I don't see. You know me, what else do you need to know?"

"Where you live, what your family's like, what kind of records you have, what kind of books you read. I think it's nice to see people in their native environment."

"I have a complete collection of Prince," he said promptly. "Does that make you feel better?"

"Why couldn't I just come by your house sometime to pick you up? That way I could meet your folks. Is there some reason why I can't come over to your house? Is there some big secret here, or what?"

His face clouded. "I just don't want to talk about it, Sam."

"Some terrible family problem or something?"

"I told you I don't want to talk about it."

"I understand," she said in a rush of sympathy. Maybe she had done the wrong thing to bring up the question of his family. Poor Pip—he probably had one of those families like the ones her mother worked with at the Division of Social Services where people threw beer bottles at each other.

Pip drew closer to Sam, nuzzled her ear and then kissed her cheek softly. Sam could feel tears welling up in her eyes when she thought about how hungry for warmth he was and how brave, bearing all those family troubles by himself. Impulsively she put her arms around him and hugged him.

The next day, when Sam saw Marcy at gym, she could tell Marcy was still annoyed. "Did you and Pip have a nice lunch yesterday?'' Marcy asked, bending to pull on her socks. "I had an absolutely terrific time with Toni telling me all about the six deeply tanned lifeguards she got to know this summer."

"I'm only trying to show Pip around a little," said Sam guiltily. "It's awfully confusing around here at first for somebody new."

Mrs. Riggs blew the whistle while Sam was still struggling into her shorts, and Marcy jumped up and began galloping toward the gym.

"Meet me at Fino's after school?" Sam called after her.

"Okay." Marcy shot a smile over her shoulder.

Sam wished Marcy would get to know Pip. It would be so much easier if Marcy and Luke liked him.

That afternoon Sam got to Fino's before Marcy. She had come just to show Marcy that Pip's being in her life didn't mean she had given up her friends, so it seemed ironic, then, that once she sat down, Pip was all she could think about. She slumped in a dark booth and began shredding a paper napkin with her fingers in some agitation. She had imagined that when she started feeling really attracted to a boy it would be like being given a diamond necklace, something to show off and be proud of. She hadn't expected she would feel uneasy and guilty about it like this.

It was not as if Pip were the first boy Sam had ever been out with. She had known her share of boys, but it had always been very much along the lines of "Let's go for pizza with the guys." No long looks. No touching under the table. Sam had never been into heavy relationships. She was a lighthearted, sociable type of creature. She couldn't understand what had happened that she was spending her lunchtime at the Wishing Tree with Pip. She only knew that what she had told Marcy—that she was just helping him find his way around—was not strictly true. The fact was she liked to be near Pip, and that in itself was a little puzzling. He wasn't her type. As a rule she preferred funny guys who were good dancers, guys that Marcy and Luke liked almost as much as she did, guys that fit in easily with her crowd. She had never been interested before in a boy who didn't click with her friends. And yet here was Pip—she was drawn to him like those iron filings to the magnet in chemistry class.

She pulled her spiral-bound notebook out of her purse and stared at it, prepared to make some fine resolution to make herself feel better, but she couldn't even think of one. If the thing with Pip had gotten too intense for her, it might make sense to arrange things so that the two of them would be around other people more until she felt sure of her feelings. But so far Pip hadn't made any friends of his own, and as cool as Marcy and Luke were toward him you couldn't blame him for not wanting to hang around with them. And maybe it wasn't the intensity that was bothering her, anyway. Maybe it was just the disapproval she picked up from Luke and Marcy. Was she turning out to be some sort of conformist slave, one of those pathetic types who couldn't do anything her friends didn't like?

She lifted her red marker, and to her previous resolutions she now added, "3. Be true to myself." She felt comforted by getting that fine sentiment down in red ink, even though what it meant was not so obvious yet. Her list seemed to be losing its power to make sense of things. This thing with Pip seemed to be too big and too complicated to fit on a list.

The bell on Fino's door rang, and Sam heard a bunch of girls streaming in, talking loudly. They squeezed into the booth behind Sam and began a consultation about pizza toppings. "Okay," Happy's clear treble voice rose above the babble. "Green pepper, sausage, pepperoni and extra cheese. That's settled. Monique, you go up and order it." Monique's shoes scuffed noisily against the floor as she slid out of the booth.

"Monique is such a sweet girl," said Happy when the sound of Monique's footsteps had receded. "And when she looses twenty pounds and gets those braces off, she's going to be really attractive. A lot of boys like that busty, sort-of-overdone look."

Sam slumped lower down in her booth, not wanting Happy to see her. She had a lot on her mind and was in no mood to exchange pleasantries with Happy. One thing was clear in Sam's mind—had she been Monique, she would have made sure Happy was the one to go order the pizza. That was the only way to stop Happy from cutting you the minute you were out of hearing. Cutting was like a reflex with her. But the girls in the next booth might not know that yet. They were sophomores, probably. Sam had not yet recognized any of their voices.

"Danny Barnes likes Monique just the way she is now," said one girl rebelliously. She had a rather low and gravelly voice, and Sam had to strain to hear her.

"He's taking her to the Petite Marmite Saturday night. She told me so."

Incredulous sighs rounded the booth. "I hear it's awfully romantic there," said one girl. "And expensive. Lucky Monique."

"Oh, well, Danny Barnes," said Happy disparagingly. "I wouldn't call Danny Barnes a real date, would you?"

"So who would you call a real date, then?" said the gravelly voice.

"Jake Furlong, Jim Shipman—"

"And Luke Lancaster," breathed another girl. "Gorgeous Luke Lancaster. You're so lucky, Happy, running with that popular crowd, knowing all those absolutely spectacular guys. All the guys I know are so immature and so, well, creepy."

A spate of giggling engulfed the table.

"I may go around with that crowd," Happy said, "but I'm not really one of them, if you know what I mean."

You can say that again, thought Sam. Hardly any of us can stand you.

"I maintain my objectivity," Happy went on. "I can see that those people are plastic. Like Samantha Morrison. Smiles and this great show of being ever so nice to everybody, but what does it mean? Zip. Because underneath that Kewpie doll face is nothing. She doesn't have a thought in her little head. We're talking a girl who can't walk and chew gum at the same time."

Sam's ears burned. She slid even further down and covered her eyes with her hand. This was getting sticky. Not that she was surprised to hear Happy libeling her. They had never had any use for each other. But it had hit her suddenly that there was a certain awkwardness in her situation. It was too late to reveal her presence now. What was she going to do when Marcy came in looking for her? How was she going to escape from the booth without Happy realizing that Sam had heard every word of what had been said? Maybe she could hide under the table. When Marcy came in and didn't see her, she would just think Sam had forgotten their agreement to meet. This is what I get for eavesdropping, Sam thought.

"And then there's Marcy McNair," Happy's voice went on relentlessly. She was evidently set on criticizing everybody she knew. It sounded to Sam as if she might be going in reverse alphabetical order.

"Marcy's awful smart," said Val Adams, at last a voice Sam knew. Val was a cheerleader who, in spite of doing cartwheels and handstands, maintained enameled nails that were almost an inch long. It occurred to Sam that it might have been their common interest in the fine points of fingernail maintenance that drew Happy and Val together. "You've got to give Marcy that," Val went on. "She's got the highest grade point average in the student body, if not in the entire world. It's, like, incredible. And the big words she uses! Sometimes I don't always even understand what she's saying."

"Oh, she's smart," said Happy, in the tones of one discovering an embezzlement. "But in my opinion she's a sick, sick girl. I ask you, is it healthy to be totally fixated on grades like that?"

"Now, have I got this straight?" asked a girl. "Isn't Samantha the best friend of that brain, Marcy? Isn't it funny that somebody so smart hangs around with somebody so dumb?"

"She likes feeling superior," said Happy. "The way those three—Luke, Marcy and Samantha—hang around together, it's practically perverted. I call them Bod, Brain and Bimbo."

Everyone at Happy's table laughed. Sam did not find the quip particularly funny.

"Gee, it's really neat to get in on the ground floor like this, to find out what all these people are really like," said one girl. "You know, I thought none of the juniors and seniors were even going to speak to us at first, but then you were so friendly, Happy, and I thought, well, Lee High isn't going to be so bad after all."

"I think it's just awful about you not getting newspaper editor," said another girl whose voice Sam didn't recognize. "I mean, Luke may be good-looking, but I hear his grades are terrible. I figure the only reason they gave it to him is just because he's a boy."

"It's always that way," said the gravelly voice. "Boys get everything, and there's nothing anybody can do about it."

"Oh, I think I can do something about it," said Happy. "I've got a plan."

The bell on the door tinkled.

"Why, Marcy!" Happy exclaimed. "Look, girls, it's Marcy. Do you want to try to squeeze in here with us? We could steal a chair from one of the tables. No problem at all. Come and sit with us.''

Sam knew that if Marcy walked over to Happy's table she would spot Sam cowering in the next booth, so she had no choice but to reveal her presence. She sat up and sheepishly waved at Marcy. She felt her smile growing wobbly when she met Happy's cool gray eyes.

''Sam,'' cooed Happy, her smile stretching her lips into a tight band of red. ''Why, I didn't see you over there in the next booth. Auditioning for a job with the CIA?'' Her laugh tinkled.

''Gee, I didn't see you, either,'' said Sam. ''I was just so engrossed in my book, I guess I hardly knew what was going on.''

''Your algebra book,'' said Happy, peering over into Sam's booth. ''Of course. How often I have sat enraptured by the beauty of an equation.''

The other girls giggled and looked embarrassed. Sam was glad she wasn't a boy. She supposed if she had been a boy she would have been compelled to demand an explanation from Happy of what she had overheard, and then she would possibly have to punch Happy out, which was not her style at all. It was easier to pretend nothing had happened and bide her time.

A few minutes later, as Sam and Marcy stood at the counter waiting for their turn to order two personal-size pizzas, Marcy said, ''Happy didn't seem exactly delighted to have you sitting in the next booth, did she?''

Sam rolled her eyes. "You should have heard it, Marce. She was cutting us to ribbons. She actually called Luke, you and me, Bod, Brain and Bimbo."

Marcy giggled. "Not bad." She glanced at Sam. "Not that you're a bimbo, Sam, but—"

Sam cut her off. "You don't think I'd let anything Happy said about me get to me, do you? I know plain-out jealousy when I hear it. Not that it cheers me up any to have her brainwashing every sophomore she can get hold of and telling them how awful we are, but it's basically not important. The big thing is that she was plotting against Luke! If you'd been another five minutes late I would have probably heard the whole thing. She was saying she had figured out a way to get to be editor."

"Showing off for those girls, probably. I saw that they were almost all sophomores. I suppose Happy's doing her I'm-totally-democratic routine. You'd think they'd be a little bit suspicious of a girl who even wears shoulder pads in her sweatshirts."

"Don't you even wonder what her plan is?"

"I hate to say it, but I think we're going to find out all too soon."

But Marcy was mistaken. The next day at the first newspaper staff meeting of the year, Happy's intentions seemed even more mysterious, at least to Sam.

Mr. Perkins shifted his position at the table to signal that he was about to begin. He was a large, Buddhalike man, fat, with round rimless glasses. Sam soon realized that he was using exactly the same pep talk he had used last year.

"We've got another challenging year ahead, people," he said. "There do not happen to be any seniors on this year's *Traveler*, but nevertheless, we have plenty of experienced staffers returning from last year, and last, but not least, our typists, Tracy and Danita. All of you fine people did splendid work for us last year, and we expect more of the same this year. In addition, we have a full quotient of bright new faces. Although these new staffers have a lot to learn, they bring that quality of energy and enthusiasm that keeps us all on our toes. All of you have been carefully selected, and I have no hesitation in saying I think we have a good chance of making this our best year yet."

Sam listened with only half an ear. She had heard it all before. What could Happy be planning? she wondered, watching her. From her shell-pink fingernails to the twin pearls on each earlobe, Happy gave an impression of cool control. She might have just stepped out of some hermetically sealed container except that, as Sam noted with satisfaction, the humidity had frizzled her artfully tousled hair. It was impossible to read her eyes.

"As some of you know," Mr. Perkins went on, "I believe in giving the students full responsibility for getting the newspaper out. Only in this way can you learn and grow. I will, of course, be on hand every day to help with any problems and to make sure the newspaper doesn't break the laws on criminal libel." He produced a half smile.

Sam knew that soon he would retire to his corner desk where he would mark homework papers. Mr.

Perkins belonged to the laissez-faire school of faculty advisers.

"Now, before I turn the floor over to Luke," he said, "are there any questions?"

There were never any questions. Even sophomores knew better than to ask questions that could only lead to long boring answers.

Happy raised her hand. Mr. Perkins looked surprised. "Yes, Happy?"

"Mr. Perkins, I just want to share what I've been hearing around school lately," she said.

"We've only been in school two days," muttered Marcy. "So what has she got? A Harris poll?"

"I have sensed this concern," Happy went on, "that the newspaper staff is not truly representative of the writing talents in this school. I've even heard people say that the newspaper staff is nothing but an in-crowd enclave."

"An in-crowd enclave?" repeated Mr. Perkins blankly.

"An enclave is a kind of closed group," Happy explained.

"I know what an enclave is, Happy," he said, repressively. "I was only surprised at what you said. I believed it to be generally known that the newspaper staff is chosen on the basis of submitted writing samples."

"But that's just it, Mr. Perkins," Happy said. "It's the newspaper staff that does the choosing. What people are saying is that if the staff reads a sample and if it's written by somebody who they think is a geek—"

"Or a freak," Marcy put in, "or a nerd or a wimp or a burnout case or a nebbish or a space cadet or a flake or a loser." She was ticking off the terms as she went and fast running out of fingers.

Happy glared at her. "As I was saying, the feeling is that a submission like that automatically gets pitched out. I've even heard people say that last year the seniors just picked the best-looking girls."

"Why, thank you, Happy," said Marcy graciously.

"I don't know quite how to take this." Luke grinned.

"Honestly, Happy," Sam exploded. "What a bunch of junk that is. The staff is picked in a fair competition. I don't see why you're spreading such a dumb rumor."

"I'm not the one spreading it. And I didn't say I *believed* it," said Happy. "I think we all should be aware of what's being said. After all, this is a newspaper. We should be tuned in to the climate of opinion around here."

"Fine," said Mr. Perkins, casting a longing look in the direction of the stack of papers he wanted to get marked. "Well, I'm sure we can just disregard these ill-natured complaints. Now if there are no more questions, I'll just turn the floor over to Luke."

Samantha was sure Happy was laying the foundation for some sort of dirty trick, but she just couldn't imagine what it was going to be. She couldn't have figured she would get any support from Mr. Perkins for this idea that the staff selection wasn't fair. And she would need faculty help if she were going to appeal to the administration for a new selection method.

Besides, if Happy maintained the whole process was corrupt, her position on the staff would be as much in jeopardy as anyone else's, so what was the point? It wasn't as if there was any hope of her pitching Luke off and then remaining herself.

Luke sat on the table at the head of the class. "It's good to see all these new faces here this year," he said, easily. "I want to say a special hi to all you sophomores." Looking up at him, one of the new staffers lifted a hand self-consciously to smooth her hair. "Now they tell me," Luke went on, "that every speech ought to begin with a joke, so I'll start by introducing the biggest joke I know, my assistant editor, Happy Whitaker."

Happy did not act at all offended by Luke's flip introduction. She turned and smiled regally in the direction of the sophomores. "And over here on my right," Luke said, "our feature editor, Sam Morrison, and our news editor, Marcy McNair. I guess you all know that in the past the *Traveler* has been kind of on the bland side, a little too heavy with the staid point of view of the administration. I want to change all that this year. The floor is now open for suggestions."

"Change the name of the paper," Sam said at once.

"What's wrong with the *Traveler*?" asked Happy.

"I just don't think it's very dignified for a newspaper to be named after Robert E. Lee's horse," said Sam.

"If we could just confine ourselves to content right now, you guys," said Luke. "Forget the name. What we want here are some sizzling new stories, stories that really grab the gut, fast-breaking, action-packed stories.''

"Let's do one on that new rich kid," suggested Felicia promptly. "Everybody's interested in him."

"He's not even here yet," said Sam.

"Oh, yes, he is," said Tracy.

Everybody looked at her, and she blushed hotly. "He's in my chemistry class," she whispered.

"What's he like?" asked Felicia.

"Nice," whispered Tracy, looking down at her shoes.

"Is that all you can say? Nice?" said Felicia. "Is he tall or short, fat or lean, dark or blond, gorgeous or noxious? Give me a break."

"Lay off Tracy, Felicia," said Luke. "Unless, that is, you want to type all your own stories."

Tracy shot him a look of dumb gratitude.

"That story would actually come under 'Personality Profiles.''' said Sam, "That's a regular feature. Okay, it sounds interesting. Maybe we should go with that."

"I'll write it," said Felicia promptly, "since it was my idea."

Luke looked at his watch. "We're almost out of time today, folks," he said, "but next time we'll get down to some real substance, okay? Think about it."

After newspaper staff, Marcy walked with Samantha to gym. "Why did you let Felicia take that story?" she asked Sam indignantly. "You passed up a terrific opportunity. Tracy says that Byron kid is nice, and here was your chance to broaden your horizons. Broaden them beyond Pip, to be exact. You know, a couple of people have already asked me if you're going with Pip. Is that what you want? To spend all your spare time with that guy and not see another soul? Don't you want to keep some variety in your relationships?"

"You just don't understand, Marcy," said Sam. She looked around her to make sure no one was listening. "His family has a drinking problem," she whispered.

"Oh, my God," said Marcy, growing pale. "I didn't know."

"Or maybe it's a case of spouse abuse," said Sam, fair-mindedly.

"Well, make up your mind, Sam, which one is it?" said Marcy sharply.

"I'm not sure. He just let me know that he had terrible problems at home. That's why I can't go over and pick him up at his house."

"Wait a minute," said Marcy. "After he told you this, he didn't happen to kiss you, did he?"

"What does that have to do with it?"

"I thought so. It's the old sympathy ploy, and you fell for it hook, line and sinker. I'll bet the real reason you aren't supposed to pick him up at home is that he's living with another woman."

"Marcy, how did you get so cynical?" Sam stamped her foot.

"From experience," said Marcy. "I tell you, there's something fishy about that boy. Don't you think that just possibly you are seeing too much of him? At the very least, don't you think simple prudence tells you that you ought to leave him in a little doubt about your feelings? I hate to be blunt about this, Sam, but you look at him as if he were a hot-fudge sundae.''

Sam, feeling chastened, followed Marcy back into the girls' locker room where crowds of girls were changing clothes in an atmosphere steamy from showers and redolent of deodorant, hair spray and baby powder.

"Tell you what," said Marcy, her voice muffled as she slipped her jersey blouse over her head. "Felicia's article will probably be full of things that need further clarification. Then all you have to do is track down Phil Byron to check up on a few things, and you'll get to meet him."

"I expect Felicia's story will be okay," said Sam. All the same, she thought, it was an idea. She had to admit to a nagging feeling that what Marcy said made some sense. It wouldn't hurt just to meet this Byron boy.

Chapter Four

"He says he doesn't give interviews," said Felicia in a flat voice.

"Maybe you didn't put it to him right," said Marcy, looking pointedly at Sam. "Maybe one of us ought to try a different approach."

"What's he like?" asked Ingrid.

"An icicle. The world's worst snob. I expect he spends all day just talking to himself in the mirror."

"Good-looking?" suggested Happy.

Felicia shrugged. "Not particularly. Overrated, in my opinion. After he looked at me as if I were some new kind of slug, he hopped in his white Mercedes convertible and tooled away. This Byron guy is the kind who fuels Communist revolutions."

"Who cares, anyway?" said Luke impatiently. "Interviews with rich kids aren't what we need to make this paper sizzle. We've had too much concern in the past with the social angle, the surfaces. We want to get beyond that.''

Samantha was making a list. "Before you do any of that, I'd better make my regular feature assignments, Luke, and then you can sort of see where we are."

By the time Sam had sorted out the features and Marcy had tapped the people she needed to cover all the stories on her own list, Luke was seething with impatience.

"And let's not forget," Happy put in, "that the Senior Assembly is coming up next week. We're helping the Student Council with that."

"Am I the only person here who's interested in genuine, hard-nosed journalism?" Luke asked. "Why doesn't anybody have any ideas along that line? New ideas. Not the same old profiles of teachers and the volleyball team."

There was a moment of silence while Sam tried hard to think of an idea for a news story, but couldn't come up with one. She noticed everyone else's face looked equally blank except for Happy's. Happy was smiling. Sam promised herself that she would skip television that night and devote her spare time to thinking up a fresh news story. With Happy determined to undercut him, Luke was going to need hers and Marcy's full cooperation to turn the paper around.

Luke began to prod them gently. "What about a scathing look at the ineffectiveness of the new computer scheduling?" he suggested. "What about investigating how easy it is for kids to buy liquor in this town? Do any of you think you could handle stories like that?''

Sam grew rigid with anxiety at the thought of trying to buy liquor illegally. Not only would she be grounded for the rest of her natural life if she got caught, but she had the idea there were some legal penalties, too. And as for computers, she knew nothing at all about them. Glancing around her, she decided everyone else was in pretty much the same boat.

Luke reached for a pencil. ''Something I'm giving a lot of thought to is an in-depth look at whatever it is that goes into that stuff the cafeteria calls meat loaf. What do you think about that?''

Sam noticed that people were beginning to look interested. After all, they had all eaten that meat loaf.

''You see, it's not so hard to come up with an idea,'' Luke said. ''But I can't do this by myself. I want you all to come up with your own ideas for news stories. Meanwhile I'm going to start doing the spadework for a story on the cafeteria food. When you see how I put the story together, maybe you can see more the direction I want the *Traveler* to move in. I see us moving into exposés, investigations, real behind-the-scenes looks at how things work. I don't expect a revolution overnight, but that's the way I see us moving.''

''It sounds hard,'' said Felicia doubtfully.

''It's just a different approach,'' said Luke. ''Now, I want you all to start giving some real thought to this new direction of ours.''

''Yes, your majesty,'' said Happy.

A minute later when they had split up into informal groups to sketch out some questions and outlines for their assignments, Sam noticed Happy huddled in a corner with Ingrid, a pink-cheeked sophomore recruit. Sam distinctly heard Happy say "bimbo" and realized that Ingrid was staring at her. Her face burned. How could she fight being called a bimbo? Was she supposed to go around with a pencil over her ear, dropping words of three syllables to prove she had a little basic intelligence? Momentarily, a simpler solution occurred to her. She could put her fingers around Happy's throat and shake her hard.

Sam took a deep breath and tried to return her attention to her work. If she let every nasty crack Happy made get to her, she was never going to get anything done. Furthermore, she knew it would only please Happy to get a rise out of her. Not to mention that she would look pretty dumb shaking Happy and shrieking, "I am not a bimbo." To disregard what was being whispered in that corner was the only way to maintain what shreds of dignity she had left.

"I could kill Happy," Sam said grimly, as she and Marcy walked to gym together.

"That's one way to give Luke the hard-news story he's looking for. What's she been up to now?"

"Oh, she was whispering to Ingrid over by the pencil sharpener, telling her what an idiot I am. I couldn't hear every word, but the drift was pretty clear."

"Ingrid, huh? Happy's really got this thing about sophomores, doesn't she? I guess she likes to get them young and impressionable. Well, she's always been like that, Sam, whispering, pulling strings behind the scenes. Unfortunately there's never much you can call her on."

"I hate her," said Sam.

Marcy grinned. "As long as it's nothing serious. Hey, Luke is really taking this editor stuff seriously, isn't he? Did you catch that fire in his eye? I thought he was positively inspiring. I promised myself I'm going to go home and think up an original angle on a news story, which is insane because, when I stop to think about it, I need every second to study for that chemistry test." She shifted her gym bag to her other hip. "Sam, why didn't you just tell dumb Felicia that you'd take over the Byron interview if she can't handle it?"

"We can't harass Phil Byron. If he doesn't want to be interviewed, that's that. Besides, I don't exactly crave to be looked at as if I were a slug." Sam pushed open the door to the girls' locker room.

"I don't see how you can resist chasing him down if only to get a peek," said Marcy. "I'm getting curious about what he's like. Everybody's got a different slant on him. Will the real Phil Byron please stand up!"

"You're interested in Phil Byron?" Samantha made a deep bow, sweeping her gym bag along the floor. "Be my guest. You're welcome to him."

Marcy laughed. "Maybe if I weren't starting my new job this week. But okay, I'll quit bugging you about it. Probably."

That day, Sam and Pip once more ate lunch by the Wishing Tree. It was getting to be a habit with them in spite of Sam's uncomfortable feeling that she was spending too much time with Pip.

She unwrapped her cafeteria pizza from its napkin. "How are you liking your classes?" she asked, looking at Pip anxiously. "Are you meeting any new people?"

"A few," he said. He stretched out on the grass and bit into his pizza.

"You really have to make an effort to meet people when you're new," said Sam. "You know, it might be better for us to eat lunch with everybody else. That way you could get to know some other kids."

"Trying to get rid of me, Sam?"

"No! I just worry about you, that's all. I know it's tough being new."

"Don't worry about me," he said. Leaning back on one elbow he ripped off another bite of pizza with his teeth. The mozzarella stretched into threads and after a moment's suspense disappeared into his mouth. Burned brown by a summer of tennis, Pip was wearing a knit shirt of startling whiteness and weathered jeans so tightly stretched across his person that they must have threatened his circulation. To see him lying back on the grass like that, no one would ever guess that he had a sordid home life and had only just arrived at a new school. Sam decided he must be one of those "survivors" her mother spoke of, people who rose like phoenixes above the debris of their lives. The sun on his face made his dark skin golden, and Sam began to have an overpowering desire to reach out and touch his long dark eyelashes. Get a grip, she told herself. Marcy's right. You need to lighten up.

She cleared her throat. "You know, my mother is a social worker."

"Yes, I know," he said. He was looking at her cautiously.

"She might be able to put you in touch with people who could help your family."

"Look, Sam, I thought we weren't going to talk about my family."

"Don't you think that when a person likes another person he or she should share what's on his or her mind with that other person when that other person is only trying to help?"

"I'll tell you what. I'll really think over what you've just said, okay? I'll give it my serious consideration. Now, tell me about this Senior Assembly everybody's talking about."

Sam looked at him with concern, but decided it was best to go along with his obvious desire to change the subject. "Senior Assembly? Oh, that's a lot of fun. The seniors all vote on who in their class is tops. Like Most Attractive, Most Intellectual, and so on. I'm counting ballots this year because the Student Council and the newspaper staff do it together. It's a big job. Of course, we're all sworn to secrecy until the assembly, which is superdramatic. On assembly day the student-body president announces the award, and a spotlight shines on a little placard on stage. Like, say, for most attractive it would read, Linda Sherry. So then Linda Sherry shrieks, pretends to be surprised out of her mind and comes up to stand in the spotlight, next to her sign. The tension is terrific. Seniors start to give way under the pressure—you can hear the sound of people chewing their nails all over the auditorium. When it's all over everybody claps and screams, the band plays, trumpets blow. People who didn't get what they hoped for have to be helped out by their friends. It's an extremely big day for the seniors.''

"I thought they hadn't voted yet.''

"They haven't. They're supposed to vote tomorrow.''

"So you don't really know that Linda Sherry's going to get Most Attractive, then. You were just using it for an example.''

"I've got a pretty good idea of who's going to get things. It's got to be people that everybody knows, so that narrows it down to twenty or thirty kids. It's pretty easy to guess who's going to get what.''

"The in crowd cleans up, huh?''

Sam winced.

"Did I say something wrong?''

"I was just remembering something that happened in newspaper staff. It's not important.'' She was getting that burning feeling in her stomach again, and she didn't think it was the pizza. Things were not working out at all the way she had hoped. Luke was editor of the paper, all right, but she was jumpy every minute waiting to see what Happy's next move would be.

And then there was Pip. When she saw him, he lit up the landscape, everything suddenly seemed to be terrifically full of pizzazz and life itself ran at a faster pace. When he drew close to her she had to take deep breaths to keep her voice from going all squeaky. But if this was love, something important was missing.

Where was the serene happiness she had always understood was part of the package?

"If you can't finish that pizza," Pip said, "I could take it off your hands."

Sam handed the rest of it to him, then jumped to her feet. While Pip finished off her pizza, she walked over to the Wishing Tree and began reading the messages. "Thrasher skateboard, $15 or best offer," read one message. "An A in English," another implored. "If M.M. will just speak to me, I won't ask for another thing all year." So many futile wishes, thought Sam despairingly. What was the point? Nothing you wished for ever turned out the way you hoped. She plucked out a note that had been thrust between the branches. "Girl in old hat," it read. "Where have you been all my life? Meet me here after school. P.A.B. III." Sam gasped.

"You okay, Sam?" Pip asked, sitting up.

"Fine," she said. "I'm fine." She stuffed the note back in the tree and went back to Pip, her heart pounding as if she had run the sixty-yard dash. She hoped she was managing to look reasonably calm. On the other side of the tree, a tall boy in torn jeans was affixing a message with a paper clip.

"I've been thinking," Pip said. "If you're looking for a desk, the worst place to look for it is here. What you need is a secondhand store in a college town, say. Probably a lot of college students sell their desks when they graduate instead of going to the trouble of moving them. What do you think?"

"Huh?"

"Sam, did you hear anything I just said?"

"Yes, you said, 'What do you think?'"

"Is something on your mind? Want to tell me about it?"

Sam drew a ragged breath. "So much is on my mind," she said, "that I wouldn't know where to begin." She didn't see how Pip could act offended. It wasn't as if he were exactly Mr. Open-and-Honest himself.

After lunch Sam rushed to her fifth-period class, her mind in a turmoil. She tried to think of every other person she knew who wore a hat. It didn't take long. Nobody else wore a hat.

Sam was sure that the note was meant for her. And it had to have been written by Phil Byron. But if P.A.B. III was Phillip Arrington Byron III the way Sam thought, she couldn't figure out where he had seen her. She never wore her old hat to school and she didn't see how she could have missed noticing him if he were trailing her around town. White Mercedes convertibles were not exactly a dime a dozen in Fenterville.

The rest of the afternoon seemed to drag interminably. Maybe that note had been put on the tree yesterday, Sam thought in alarm, and she had already missed her chance to meet P.A.B. Or worse, maybe the note had been put on the tree today, and she hadn't.

She felt shot through with vague feelings of anxiety, but by the end of the day she knew she had to go to the Wishing Tree. If the note had been written by Phil Byron the way she thought, how could she pass up the chance to see for herself what he was like? He had only been at Lee High a few days and already he had six different reputations. She owed it to the *Traveler* to check it out. Byron was news.

Besides, going by the Wishing Tree didn't commit her to anything. She would just stand at the tree a few minutes reading the messages as if she were still keeping an eye out for an affordable desk. What could be more natural? And then if Byron came by—well, then she would see, that's all.

Luke stopped her in the hall after the final bell. "Why don't we go by Burger King or something for a minute?" he said. "I need to bounce my ideas off of somebody, and Marcy's got this new job doing research for some lawyer. She can't come."

Sam started guiltily. "I can't, either, Luke."

"It won't take long. I'm not going to talk your ear off," he said, looking a little hurt.

"Maybe you could call me tonight?"

Luke snorted. "Going someplace with that Winston guy again, huh?" He turned away.

"I'm not going anyplace with Pip!" Sam protested. Red in the face and with the uneasy feeling she was failing Luke, she made her way through the building against the surging traffic. She hadn't even tried to think up an idea for a news story in spite of her promises to herself. And what was she doing right now? Did it even make sense? She must be out of her mind.

Behind the school the picnic tables were deserted. The gym seemed unnaturally still and empty. Sam was beginning to feel it wouldn't be as easy as she had thought to saunter casually over to the Wishing Tree.

The books in her arms felt suddenly heavy, but she forced her feet to stumble in the direction of the Wishing Tree. She darted a nervous look over her shoulder. Just past the clump of trees, school buses were roaring past, yet she felt eerily alone. Maybe she should forget the whole thing.

Suddenly she heard someone behind her and whirled around.

"Pip!" she cried.

"Hi, Sam. Still looking for that desk?"

"Yes. I mean, no. Actually the fact is I sort of came here to follow up on a story for the *Traveler*."

"Oh." He sat down on the grass.

"What are you doing here?"

"I'm supposed to meet a girl here."

She swallowed. "You are?" She couldn't remember when she had felt so hurt. She felt as if there were a heavy weight on her chest, and her throat felt painfully constricted. "I guess she's late. Well, I'd better be going. I don't want to butt in on your date."

He caught her hand as she turned. "Wait up, Sam. You didn't really come here to work on a story for the *Traveler*, did you?"

Tears stung her eyes. "No," she said. She awkwardly fished a tissue out of her purse and blew her nose. "I came here to meet somebody, too." That would show him, she thought.

"Stop sniffing, Sam. The girl I came here to meet is you. I'm P.A.B. III."

"How can your initials be P.A.B.? You told me your name was Pip Winston!" she cried indignantly.

"I lied."

Sam had a momentary blinding flash of insight. She saw that she should have seized the chance to take karate lessons at the Y when they were offered last summer. Then she could have given Pip a swift chop to the back of the neck instead of standing there looking at him with her mouth open.

Pip rubbed his nose and looked at her ruefully. "When I had to come up with an alias real quick," he said, "the only thing that came into my head was the name of the competition. Winston cigarettes, you know."

"And you are Phillip Arrington Byron III?" she asked in a dangerous voice.

"Yup."

"And you don't have terrible family problems."

"Nope."

"I guess you have a car."

"A Mercedes convertible," he confessed.

"And I felt sorry for you!" she cried. "I guess you've been laughing your head off. Well, I hope you have lots of happy chuckles over it in the future when you're eating lunch alone."

She wheeled and stomped away.

"Wait up, Sam."

"Get lost," she called over her shoulder.

When Sam got home, she threw herself on the bed and cried in humiliation. Marcy had been right all the time about Pip. Sam felt not just foolish but slightly sick. Byron Tobacco, Winston cigarettes—it had been so obvious, so transparent. She should have seen through his phony name.

When she remembered the first item on her list of resolutions—"Go steady with Phillip Arrington Byron III"—her face burned with mortification. No wonder Pip's eyes had widened when he saw the list that day at the ice-cream shop. He had probably expected her to go chasing after him with a butterfly net.

Downstairs the doorbell rang. Fruitcake hated the sound of the doorbell, and he immediately began baying as if a full moon had risen. Sam looked out the front window and saw a white Mercedes convertible parked out front. She could hear Pip below hammering on the screen door to the accompaniment of Fruity's baying. She ran downstairs. "Hush, Fruity," she yelled. She threw open the door.

"I have nothing to say to you," she said.

"Is that why you came downstairs?" he said. "Come on, Sam. Don't be mad. What's the difference what my name is, huh?"

"You lied to me from start to finish."

"I did not. You jumped to a lot of conclusions."

"If there is one thing I cannot stand, it's deceit."

"Are you going to tell me you never deceived me?"

Remembering how she had shielded Luke from Pip, Sam sensed she was on shaky ground so she changed her tack. "My father is going to be home pretty soon," she said. "I wish you would go away."

"Honest? Because if you really want me to, I mean if you want me to go away for good, I will."

Sam snuffled inelegantly, and Pip handed her his handkerchief. "Why don't we go for a ride," he said. "So we can talk."

Sam certainly didn't want her father to come home to walk in on this embarrassing scene. She couldn't imagine how she would begin to explain it. That was absolutely the only reason, she told herself, that she went out and got into Pip's car.

When Pip switched the ignition on, the Mercedes leapt into action with the precision of a thousand Prussian soldiers clicking their heels simultaneously. Sam noticed that the seats were covered in what looked like real leather. She wondered why she had thought this sort of opulence would be romantic. When you considered all the people in the world who didn't have enough to eat, it was actually kind of disgusting.

"What do people call you?" she asked as they pulled away from her house. "Phil? Ari?"

He darted a surprised glance at her. "Pip. That's what my family's always called me."

Somehow, quite irrationally, that made her feel a little better.

"Look at it from my point of view, Sam. I'm new here. Before, I went to a private boys' school, St. Bartolf's. We just saw girls on the weekends, right? I don't have just heaps of practice with girls. Then practically the first day I get here one of your friends dumps mud all over me. I'm sitting there in the ice-cream shop without my lenses, I can just barely make out the shapes of things around the room, I'm drenched, my shoes are wet, I'm feeling like two cents and suddenly I spot my name on this hit list in your notebook. Naturally, I dive for cover."

"If you're trying to make me feel sorry for you again, you're wasting your time," said Sam. "I won't fall into that trap twice." Just the same, like the sudden twanging of a violin string, she got a flash of the panicky feeling Pip must have had on that first day.

"I'm not trying to make you feel sorry for me. Look, I'm the same person, you're the same person, why can't we just go on the way we were before?" he asked plaintively.

"You won't need me anymore," Sam said, looking out into the distance. "People will be all over you."

"Okay, I have noticed there are some circles where my grandfather's name and my grandfather's money count for something. They just don't happen to be the circles I want to hang around in."

"I guess you've been awarded six patents, too," said Sam glumly.

"Where'd you get that idea?"

She shrugged.

"What's Pip Winston got that Pip Byron doesn't have?" he asked, smiling at her crookedly.

"Me."

"Oh, come off it, Sam."

Tears began trickling down her cheeks, which was not exactly what she had planned.

"If I pull the car over and kiss you some, are you going to belt me?" he asked.

"Probably not," she admitted.

Pip pulled the car into the Krispy Creme parking lot, then leaned over and kissed her. Sam decided she felt a little bit better.

"I guess you're going to think I'm a pretty insubstantial person that I can't carry a grudge longer than this," she said, sniffling as she put her arm around him.

"Hey, Sam, I *like* you. Friends?"

She managed a weak smile. "Friends," she agreed.

Chapter Five

"What do you *mean* Pip is Phil Byron?" screeched Marcy.

Sam held the phone away from her ear a second until Marcy had finished screeching, then spoke once more into the receiver. "His family calls him Pip," she explained. "That's because when he was little he couldn't say Phillip. He could just say Pip."

"I refuse to believe this boy was ever little," said Marcy. "I thought you said his name was Winston. That's right, I distinctly remember your saying he was Pip Winston."

"Winston was a pseudonym, sort of like a nom de plume."

"What you mean is it was an alias, sort of like a lie."

"He wanted people to appreciate him for himself," said Sam, "and not just because of his grandfather's money, so I guess he used the name of Winston until he felt more comfortable."

"The vanity, the colossal presumption of it," said Marcy. "To just assume everybody he met was after his money! I have no patience with people like that."

"I really like him, Marcy."

"That doesn't count. That's strictly physical."

Sam didn't bother to deny it. She realized that quite possibly Marcy was right. "Just lay off him, okay?"

"Okay, Sam. You are my friend. If you really like him, I'll lay off him."

"Good."

"I knew there was something fishy about him," said Marcy, unable to resist having the last word.

Breaking the news to Luke the next morning was simpler.

"You mean to tell me this guy is really the Byron kid?"

"That's right."

"Jeez," said Luke disgustedly. "It figures."

"I guess you're wondering why he used a different name at first," said Sam, steeling herself for another awkward explanation.

"I couldn't care less, Sam. Save your breath. Jeez. A Mercedes convertible, right? My cup runneth over. Let me outa here."

"See you in newspaper staff," said Sam.

"Oh, right," said Luke, his mouth twisting ironically. "Today we count the flipping senior ballots, right?"

Sam couldn't put her finger on exactly why, but looking at Luke, she felt a fresh surge of uneasiness.

That day Pip gave Sam a ride home from school. He drove her past his house so she could see what it looked like, and she realized right away why he had never wanted her to go by there when he was going incognito. The place was three stories high, had white pillars in front like Monticello, formal gardens in back like the city arboretum and a vast lawn like a golf course. Thrown around the whole property was a low brick wall, and in front was a wrought iron gate between heavy brick pillars that were topped with matching iridescent glass balls. It had the look of a historical monument.

"My grandfather had a thing for vulgar ostentation," explained Pip. "A bit much, huh?"

"I don't suppose you have to live here, do you? You could move into someplace smaller."

"No use telling my father we don't think the place is cozy. He grew up here. He likes it."

Sam looked around. "You don't mean to tell me you walked all the way to my house from way over here."

"I parked the Mercedes a few blocks away from your house. Do we have to keep coming back to all that, Sam?"

"I'm just trying to get everything straight in my mind. Having somebody change his identity on you takes a little getting used to."

"I don't see why. Labels aren't that big a deal."

"So, did you go out and buy this car as soon as your grandfather's will was read?"

"No, I got it for my birthday. We weren't exactly living on skid row before my grandfather died, you know. My father was a partner with Blake, Henry, Fenner and Bean in D.C. I guess it's because my grandfather was such a Scrooge, but my dad doesn't believe in depriving kids of everything just because they're young, so the car was waiting outside for me the morning I turned sixteen. I guess you could say that indirectly I have my grandfather to thank for that."

"So you've always been rolling in it, huh?"

"Look, you didn't hold it against me when you thought I was hard up and my family was a wreck, did you?"

"Of course not. That's different."

"I don't see how. Why should you hold it against me that I'm not hard up and that my family is doing okay?"

Sam thought about it a minute. "I see what you mean. It's bad to be prejudiced." She fished her spiral-bound notebook out of her purse and wrote, "4. Work to overcome prejudices." When she looked up she saw that Pip was grinning at her. Blushing, she rapidly stuffed her notebook back in her purse.

"I'll have to bring you by sometime to meet my folks," he said, "but Mom's not home now. Since she knew I was having dinner with your family and Dad had to work late, she thought this was a good time to drive Terry to Raleigh to shop. We hadn't thought about how since she wasn't going to be wearing uniforms to school anymore she was going to need all new clothes."

"If you were both in private school in D.C., I'm surprised your parents didn't sign you up for the Academy."

"Well, my dad's planning to get into politics. He thinks it gives the voters a bad impression when you put your kids in private schools. It makes you come across as an elitist. You know what they say—you can go to Harvard or you can go into state politics, but not both. He won't be able to get anything off the ground for years, though. It's the sort of move you have to build up to gradually."

Back when Sam had issued the invitation for Pip to come to dinner, it had been her plan that during the meal she would urge her mother to talk about all the resources available locally to troubled families. That had seemed like a terrific idea last week. Now it turned out Pip's family wasn't troubled at all and everything was different. How would her parents react to his new identity?

That evening when Pip sat down with her family around the dinner table, Sam was on edge.

Her mother ceremoniously placed a steaming casserole dish on the table.

"White meat or dark, Pip?" Sam's father inquired.

"Dark," said Pip. "That smells terrific. What is it?"

"Just a little fricasseed chicken with mushrooms," said Sam's mother with an unconvincing assumption of modesty.

Sam had been dreading this dinner all day. Suddenly she felt she couldn't stand the suspense any longer. "Pip's been going incognito," she blurted out. "His name is really Byron. He's Ari Byron's grandson."

Pip colored a little and studied his plate.

"Was this extreme measure really necessary, Pip?" asked Sam's dad.

"When I moved into a town and found out I was practically famous, I guess I panicked a little," Pip said.

Sam's mother began placidly serving the creamed peas and onions. Sam supposed that fifteen years in social services had left her mother immune to shocks. "I'm afraid small-town gossip can take some getting used to," she said. "Ari Byron was such a major force in Fenterville that people take an extraordinary interest in his family. I always think the interest people take in their neighbors' lives is one of the nice things about small town life, but I can see how it could be a little unnerving."

Sam was almost disappointed that her parents didn't make more of a fuss about Pip's being an impostor. Where was the moral indignation? Now that she thought of it, her parents had always erred on the side of tolerance. They weren't even down on Luke, which was ridiculous when you thought of it. Didn't they have any standards? Of course, she wanted her parents to like Pip. Naturally, she did. But she supposed she was still annoyed at bottom. She liked Pip too much to stay really mad at him, but it wouldn't have broken her heart to hear someone else giving him a little grief. In fact, it seemed only fair that somebody should.

The phone rang, and Sam's father rose to go get it. "It's for you, Sam," he said when he returned.

Sam went into the kitchen and picked up the phone. "Hi, Marilyn... Gee, I'd tell you in a minute if it were up to me," she said, "but we've been sworn to secrecy.... Since you ask, I'd wear something nice.... Yes, I think a dress would be very appropriate.... Okay, so long."

"Can't you tell your friends not to call during the dinner hour, Sam?" her mother said when Sam got back to the table.

"That wasn't my friend, Mom," Sam said. "It was just a senior trying to worm it out of me how the ballot count went."

"I thought you said everybody knew already who had won," said Pip.

"People may think they know, but they can't really be sure," said Sam. "I guess some of the more nervous types want reassurance."

"But aren't the results supposed to be a big secret?" asked her mother.

"Sure. And if it got out that I'd leaked the ballot results, Happy would have my head on a plate. She thinks Senior Assembly is sacred. What I tried to do with Marilyn was sound sort of soothing without actually saying anything definite." The phone rang again. "I'll get it," Sam said, getting up. "I'm beginning to think Luke is right. This whole Senior Assembly business stinks."

It was Tony Ashe, starting quarterback for the Lee High Rebels. He began by saying that Sam was probably surprised to be hearing from him.

"Well, no, I'm not actually *that* surprised to be hearing from you," she said. She listened to him awhile, then said, "I'd tell you in a minute if it were up to me, Tony, but I've sort of taken a blood oath of secrecy. All I can say, and I believe I can say this without betraying any confidence, is if I were you I'd wear a clean shirt."

After Tony hung up, Sam held down the receiver button a minute, then laid the receiver on the counter.

She returned to the table. "That'll be the last call for a while. I took the phone off the hook."

"I can understand the kids get a kick out of this assembly," said Sam's dad, helping himself to the creamed peas and onions. "But I can't understand why they let themselves get worked up this way. I wish people cared as much about their history grades! After all, it's not as if a person's future depends on whether or not he's voted Most Attractive."

"Are you kidding, Dad? A full page to yourself in the annual? Stack that up against having to stand there during Senior Assembly with a plastic smile on your face while all your friends go up on stage without you."

"I acknowledge my error," said Sam's dad gravely.

In a way Sam was glad the dinner had gone so smoothly, but she was, she realized, suffering from a sense of letdown. Her dramatic announcement of Pip's identity had fizzled, for one thing. Her parents had taken it all so calmly, she almost wondered if they had given the matter their full attention.

Another thing—she had realized that here her life was at last brushing against the stuff of storybooks—an heir, a fortune, an old mansion, an imposter—yet everyone kept on eating chicken and talking about Senior Assembly as if nothing out of the ordinary had happened at all. It was a trifle disillusioning. Was it possible that these things were romantic only in books and that when examined closely they were no more exciting than the weekly grocery list? Maybe it was only because she was feeling a little low, but she was starting to think that *everything* was mundane and ordinary. She had the dismal conviction that if she had been dining with Lancelot and Guinevere, they would have only sat about complaining of the mildew in the castle.

Chapter Six

After the dinner table was cleared, Fruitcake paced the kitchen floor whimpering, his nails clicking against the vinyl tiles.

"Don't give him anything, Sam," her mother warned her. "Dr. Briggs said he needs to take off five pounds. I'm supposed to measure his food, and we need to take him for some long walks, too. Look at him. He's fat as a pig."

"We could take him for a walk," Pip said softly.

Sam glanced at him. "Yes, Pip and I could take him for a walk right now."

"Sure," said Pip.

"Well, all right," said her mom.

Pip had an unerring instinct for ways to be alone together, Sam thought. She liked the idea of their being alone together herself, but it hadn't occurred to her that the simplest way would be to take Fruity for a walk.

When she took Fruity's leash off the nail in the pantry, he threw himself around in such an agony of excitement that he knocked over a pickle jar.

Sam finally succeeded in getting the leash clipped to his collar, but before she had a chance to get a hold on the end of the leash, he tore off. Sam and Pip caught up with him at the screen door, and this time Sam was careful to wrap the leash firmly around her hand before they opened the door. As the beagle galloped down the front steps of the porch, Sam was hard-pressed to keep her footing.

"Whoa, Fruity," she protested, pulling on the leash sharply. "Cut that out." Romance bites the dust again, she thought. It was hard to imagine Pip whispering endearments in her ear while she was having to rein in a wild beagle. Not that she precisely wanted Pip to—wait a minute. Oh, yes she did, she thought. She did want Pip to say sweet things to her even though he had told her a thousand lies, even if Marcy and Luke hated him. Sam was uncomfortably aware that she was not making a lot of sense right at the moment.

"We just need to tire him out some," said Pip.

It was not yet dark. Overhead the sky was a washed-out violet. The sidewalk of Mulberry Street was punctuated at intervals with the glow of street lights. Next door a column of black smoke rose from the backyard barbecue grill and faded out gray against the sky.

Sam firmly discouraged Fruity from running toward the smell of cooking steak in the Nicholsons' backyard. Luckily he was already feeling the results of his exertions after years of a sedentary life and was panting heavily and slowing his pace to a more sedate walk.

Sam glanced at Pip. His hands were thrust in his jeans pockets, and he was looking down at the sidewalk.

"The parents didn't seem to hold it against you that you were an impostor, did they?" Sam said. She hadn't intended to say that, but it just came out.

"You don't have to sound disappointed."

"I have this funny feeling that you're going to end up being one of those Teflon types," said Sam. "You know, the kind of person no mud sticks to."

"No fair. Think of the way we met! Nope it's just that your parents could see my point of view, that's all. What do they care whether I call myself Byron or Winston? I'm still the same person."

That wasn't the first time Pip had said something like that, Sam realized. She almost wondered if the one he was trying to convince was himself. It was as if he were trying to persuade himself that being Ari Byron's grandson was going to make no difference at all in his life.

What about her? Did it make any difference to her? Sam asked herself. She didn't think so, but she wasn't sure. Her attraction to Pip was so new she hadn't even gotten used to it yet, much less understood it. She couldn't tell whether his turning out to be one of the Byrons was going to change things between the two of them or not.

"You didn't know your grandfather, did you?" asked Sam hesitantly. "I mean, I heard your father and he didn't get along."

"I knew him, all right," said Pip. "He used to come see us a couple of times a year. He'd call up and tell us when he was coming. Right away the whole house would be in an uproar. I'd hear Mom saying, 'If it upsets you that much, don't invite him,' and Dad would yell, 'I don't invite him, Isobel! He just comes!'

"Just to give you an idea—one time, I was only six or seven, I had to get up from the dinner table early to go to a birthday party. I forgot to ask to be excused, and Grandfather got so mad he fell out of his chair. Okay, I know it sounds funny, Sam, but believe me it was scary, this old guy crashing down, the flailing arms and legs. Mom turned white as a sheet and hurried me out of the dining room. I could hear Grandfather roaring as I ran out of the house. The term 'ungovernable rage' was made for my grandfather."

"Gee, and all this time I thought he never spoke to any of you! I thought you'd been completely cut off. That's what the newspaper story sort of hinted at. You know, 'the surprise announcement that Philip Byron, Jr. would return to assume leadership,' and all that."

"Cut off? We should have been so lucky. That rumor was just grandfather's way of keeping all those next under him fighting among themselves, hoping to get a shot at the top. He liked that kind of thing. If you want to know the truth, I hated him."

Sam looked at him in surprise.

"Why should you be surprised about that? He was one of those people who want to tell you even how to *breathe*. I had a teacher like that at St. Bartolf's. I can't stand that type." Pip paused a minute. "I think the thing about him that got to me the most was that when he came in the house, my father would shrink. My father's six two, but he would seem to just—get smaller. I thought he was afraid. I see now that wasn't all that was going on; I mean, the guy was his father, after all, but Grandfather would show up and right away start criticizing everything in sight—Dad's haircut, his shirt, the way he made his living, us kids, the house. My father never said a thing. He would just stand there looking ashamed of himself. One time when I was twelve, I got so mad I tried to stand up to Grandfather." He laughed shortly. "I can still feel the cold fear in the pit of my stomach. For a minute there I thought he was going to hit me or have a stroke or something. Anyway, after that, I pretty much managed to be out of the house when he came. I'd go stay with friends or something."

Sam realized that as unpleasant as Pip's grandfather sounded, she was glad to be hearing about him. It was good to be at last getting a little inside Pip's mind. Somehow it seemed important for her to really get to know him.

"Do you think maybe the reason your father didn't tell your grandfather off was because of the money?"

"No," he said shortly.

"I just thought—"

"We had plenty of money," said Pip.

It occurred to Sam that there was a difference between "plenty of money" and a fortune that would make you independent and powerful for life. Such a fortune might come in handy for someone with political ambitions. She wondered if Pip's not seeing this was part of his refusal to admit that being Ari Byron's grandson was going to change his life. After all, if none of that was important, if labels didn't count and money didn't matter, why had Pip refused to let Felicia interview him? Why had he lied about his name?

They walked for a while without speaking. Sam looked over at Pip, letting her eyes linger on his face, on his cheekbones, on his skin as it darkened in the dusk. Felicia might think Pip's looks were overrated, but Sam loved the way he looked. She understood for the first time now how mothers could look at red, squalling babies and find them beautiful. Beautiful is not a look, Sam thought with a sense of surprise. Beautiful is a feeling.

Only a faint glow of light remained in the sky, as if it were a fading television screen. Under the trees and in the gutters, between the houses and on the street darkness had gathered. They had covered a lot of distance, and ahead they could make out the dark hulk of Lee High with its sprawling wings.

Fruity strained at the leash. Then he lifted his head and began to bay. "Hush, Fruity," said Sam. She pulled on his leash. "What can be the matter with him? I thought he had calmed down. I wonder if he sees a cat."

"Look, Sam," said Pip suddenly. "Over there, up on the roof."

Sam looked up, startled, and followed Pip's gaze. Across the street she could just make out a half-crouched figure moving quickly over the flat rooftop of the Lee Auditorium. Briefly the figure was silhouetted against the darkening sky.

"My God, it's a burglar," said Sam, grabbing Pip's arm. Fruity lifted his head and bayed, his throat swelling. "Do you think we should call the police?"

The figure had disappeared as suddenly as it appeared. Fruity began running back and forth, whimpering.

"The guy's gone," said Pip. "I can't see him anymore. I don't think he's still up there."

They stood there, straining to see the rooftop, when suddenly a car sped out of the student parking lot and roared right past them.

Pip swore. "I know that car! It's that old green Pontiac."

"Let's not call the police," Sam said.

"I knew you were going to say that. It's Luke's car, isn't it?"

Sam's heart sank. What could Luke have been up to? Nothing good, she was sure. She remembered how he had ridiculed the Senior Assembly. "He must have been sabotaging the assembly somehow."

The sound of Luke's car had died away. Now the street seemed strangely silent as they stood staring at the building across the street.

"I don't see how he can have sabotaged it," said Pip. "The assembly's not until tomorrow. You don't think he's set off a time bomb! Tell you what, Sam. I think we'd better call the police."

"Let's just go over there and see what he did." Sam handed Pip the leash and started across the street with determination.

"What do we care what he's done?" Pip protested. Fruity strained at the leash to follow, and Pip finally gave in and went after her.

The auditorium was a large, graceless cement-block building with high windows and a flat roof. At first glance it seemed as impregnable as a fortress.

"I wonder how he got in?" Sam said. She stared up at the roof.

"Probably slid through that air-conditioning vent up there," said Pip. "He's not very big."

"Do you think you can boost me up to the roof? If he can get through that vent, I can."

"You're out of your mind. I'm always reading in the paper about burglars getting stuck in those things. Try to imagine explaining to the police how you happened to get stuck in the air-conditioning vent. Worse, imagine explaining it to your parents. Forget it. Let's go."

"Luke just doesn't think," wailed Sam. "He doesn't consider the consequences."

"He's not the only one," muttered Pip.

"You won't boost me up to the roof?"

"You bet I won't."

"Okay, just boost me up as far as those windows. You see that window up there that's not quite closed? I think I can pry it open. I could get in through there."

"That's what I'm afraid of."

"Just boost me up on your shoulders."

"I don't want to get involved, Sam. The guy is crazy."

Sam began to feel desperate. If she couldn't get inside that auditorium and check up on what Luke was up to she didn't know what she would do. "Will you do it for *me*?" she pleaded. "All I'm asking is for you just to boost me up."

Pip hesitated a minute. "I know I'm going to regret this."

He bent down, and Sam climbed up on his shoulders. In order to pick Sam up, Pip had had to let go of Fruity's leash, and the dog began running in frantic circles around them. It was obvious that Fruity had an even lower opinion of these goings-on than did Pip, because when Pip stood up with Sam sitting on his shoulders, Fruity yelped in alarm and then began to bay desperately.

"Hush, Fruity," Sam said. She was steadying herself against the cement block wall with both hands. "Okay, now, stand very still. I'm going to try to straighten up." Sam began to wish she had cheerleading experience. To all those people who were used to tottering on top of human pyramids, this maneuver would have been child's play.

Bracing herself against the building, she unsteadily got to her feet so that she was standing on Pip's shoulders.

"I'm not too heavy, am I?" she asked anxiously.

"No, but just be careful," he said. "And speed it up. What if somebody comes by and sees us?"

Holding her breath, Sam put both hands under the metal frame of the louvered glass and pushed upward. For a fearful second she felt she might have lost her balance, but then to her relief the window creaked open.

She pushed the screen through. Then she boosted herself up on her hands to the window and wiggled through, scraping her back against the open louvre as she squeezed through the window. Her eyes were not adjusted to the relatively greater darkness of the interior, and she was not sure how far a drop it was to the floor. After she twisted her body around, she held on tight to the metal window frame and let herself down inside gradually. When she was stretched to her full length against the inside wall, her feet still did not touch the floor. She shut her eyes and forced herself to let go. She fell a short distance to the floor, landing with a clatter on the screen she had pushed in. Although she had tumbled to her knees, she wasn't hurt and quickly scrambled up again. Brushing her scraped hands against her jeans, she took a deep breath. Outside, she could hear the voice of a beagle in a state of advanced hysteria.

As she looked around her, Sam's heart skipped a beat. The auditorium looked very different in the darkness. Tonight it could have been the setting for *The Phantom of the Opera*. An exterior light shone through the window, casting a pale parallelogram of light onto the stage, but that pale patch seemed only to emphasize the darkness of the rest of the place. The folded up seats were dark shadows in the cavernous room, and the curtains on either side of the stage hung like black shrouds.

Even the atmosphere seemed different, Sam thought, shivering. The place had a funny smell to it.

All at once it came to her what Luke had been up to. What she smelled was wet paint. Moving carefully in the darkness, she approached the front of the auditorium and began mounting the steps to the stage. As she reached the top of the stairs, something hard rolled under her foot and made her stumble. She recovered her balance, but had to stand still for a minute, waiting to catch her breath. She wished she could have turned on a light switch, but she knew she dared not call attention to her presence.

She stooped and groped around on the floor with her fingers. Soon her fingers found what she had stumbled over, a large flashlight with a handle. She did not stop to wonder what a flashlight was doing on the stage. She just pressed the switch, and a beam of light shone out. That single beam of light seemed to dissipate the creepy feel of the dark auditorium at once. The faint smile of relief left her lips, however, when the beam fell upon one of the placards standing on the stage. Instead of reading Marilyn Broadhurst the way it should have, it read Marilyn the Broad. As Sam turned her beam to the other signs, she perceived that this was the mildest of the changes. She was amazed to see how easily, with fairly minor alterations, the seniors' names could be turned into rude or obscene words. Luke had changed every single name into a version that was roughly equivalent to the name, but X-rated.

"Yuck," she said aloud. Her flashlight caught a round piece of metal that shone like brass, and when

Sam walked over to it to investigate, she discovered an overturned spray-paint can. Now she could see how he had done it. He had painted over the original sign with white spray paint. When that was reasonably dry, he had written his own version of the seniors' names on with broad bands of black marker. She could still faintly make out the original lettering of the signs under his coating of spray paint.

She played the flashlight beam over the signs once more while she tried to figure out what to do. It was out of the question to leave things as they were. Some people would probably think what had happened was funny, but Sam did not think the seniors whose names had been mutilated would find it at all amusing. They would feel hurt and humiliated. Anyone would. The entire Senior Assembly would be turned into a smutty farce.

"Sam, are you all right in there?" Pip's voice came through the open window. Fruity had given up baying and was whimpering like a beagle who had been heartlessly abandoned. Sam could hear the jingling of the chain of his leash.

Hurrying down from the stage, Sam moved along the side aisle of the auditorium and unlocked the fire exit. She stuck her head out. "I'm over here, Pip. I may need help."

Fruity had already spotted her at the door and was pulling Pip over to the fire exit. "Come on in," she said. "Tie Fruity to the door handle here."

"Where did you find that flashlight?"

"It was just lying on the stage floor. Come on. Look what's happened."

Pip reluctantly followed her. He had evidently decided he preferred being in on it to standing outside wondering what was happening. He made no more protests about not wanting to get involved. He followed her up the stairs to the stage and watched as she shone the flashlight on the signs.

"Cripes," said Pip. "That's torn it. I don't see what we can do about all this."

Fruity, upon discovering he was securely tied to the door handle, objected with a peremptory bark that echoed in the dark auditorium.

Sam jumped at the sound, but she could not afford to take the time to quiet Fruity. She shook the can of spray paint, listening to the metal ball inside. "The can's not empty," she said. She put the flashlight down on the floor and squirted some paint onto the sign nearest her. "Okay," she said, "see if you can find the black marker he used. All we have to do is spray all the signs white and them rewrite them."

"*All* we have to do?"

Sam was already spraying. Pip took the flashlight from her in order to scan the floor for the marker. Without the light, Sam was conscious that her aim with the spray can was much more erratic, but she couldn't stop work. There was no time to lose. If she and Pip didn't get home pretty soon, her parents were going to start to worry.

"I've found the marker," Pip said finally.

"Here," said Sam. "You take over the spraying. I'll go behind you, rewriting the names the way they're supposed to be. Golly, I hope I can remember how to spell everybody's name." The thought that she might get one of the honors mixed up horrified her but she tried to keep calm. Luckily, she had a good memory, and the first names had generally been retained unchanged, so that was a help.

She could hear the steady squirt of Pip's spray can behind her as she went about her work. Her lettering was not as precise or as clear as she would have liked, but there was not much she could do about that. These people were lucky to have any sort of rehabilitative effort at all.

"I can't believe I'm doing this," Pip muttered. "*Why* am I doing this?"

"Kindness of heart," supplied Sam.

It seemed to take forever. Sam began to wish that senior honors were not dispensed so widely. With so many categories and with a boy and girl in each category, she began to feel as if they were going to be there all night.

Finally, Pip said, "I think that's the last of them."

As soon as they had finished, they went to untie Fruity. He stood on his hind legs and licked their faces wetly in his appreciation.

"We're going to have to stuff this empty spray can and the marker down the first storm sewer we see," said Pip, "so we don't get caught with any evidence."

"I guess Luke had to leave the stuff behind because of climbing back up out the shaft," said Sam. "He should have gone out the fire door like us." She threw the door open.

"Maybe he doesn't have your natural aptitude for crime," Pip said.

As they walked toward the street, Sam became aware that her fingers were sticking together. "Oh, dear," she said. "I got that paint on my hands."

"Me, too," said Pip. "I guess I got it on me when I was steadying the signs with my left hand."

Under the first streetlight, they paused to examine the damage to their hands. "We'll have to go out in the garage and clean our hands off with paint thinner before we go back in the house," said Sam.

Pip was looking at the handle of the flashlight. "Hey, Sam, look at this."

"The flashlight?"

"Yeah, look at the handle."

Sam saw the glimmer of a band of shiny plastic and then made out Luke's last name stamped on it.

"The flashlight's got his name on it?" she exclaimed incredulously.

"This guy *wants* to get caught."

"He's careless. He just doesn't think." She sucked on one of her painted fingers. "Golly, I hope the mineral spirits will take it off," she said. "The paint's practically dry already. We'd better clean that flashlight off, too. And strip off the name label."

They turned away from the light and began walking back toward Sam's house. "That Luke's going to be awfully disappointed tomorrow morning," Pip said. Sam could hear the satisfaction in his voice.

Chapter Seven

When Pip and Sam walked in the front door of Sam's house, they found her father sitting in the lamplight, reading the newspaper. He had taken off his shoes and had propped his stockinged feet up on a hassock. "That was some walk you two took," he commented. "You were gone long enough."

"Mom said Fruity needed to get more exercise," Sam reminded him.

Sam's dad lifted his head curiously. "Do you smell that?" he asked.

"No. No, do you smell anything, Pip?" said Sam, starting guiltily.

"I think I'll just go wash my hands," said Pip, his voice sounding grim.

"Maybe I'll do that, too," said Sam.

"It smells like mineral spirits," said Sam's dad. "That's funny. Nobody's been doing any painting, have they?"

Not waiting for her father's further speculations, Sam scuttled quickly away in the direction of the bathroom. In the kitchen, Fruity could be heard loudly slurping water out of his water bowl.

"You don't have to take him quite so far next time," Sam's dad called after her.

Later on, when Sam was bidding Pip goodbye out by his car, she noticed regretfully that the smell of paint thinner still clung to their clothes.

"You know what I think?" Pip said, opening the car door. "I think people ought to let this Luke lunatic fall flat on his face. When he has to live with the consequences of what he does, maybe he'll learn to shape up."

"It would have been awful for all those innocent seniors," Sam pointed out.

"I suppose so."

"I guess Luke thought it was funny," said Sam doubtfully.

"It *was* funny, in a heartless kind of way."

"He just doesn't think."

"Don't give me that," said Pip. "Look, do I get a good-night kiss, or does the idea of kissing a guy who's smelling of paint thinner sort of turn you off?"

Sam bent and kissed him good-night.

"Pip, thanks," she said.

She was relieved to see that he was smiling a little as he drove off.

* * *

The next morning in assembly, the president of the student council, Ronnie Miller, appeared at the podium at the side of the stage to begin the announcements. Beside Sam, Luke was sitting very still, staring at the stage.

"The senior class awards," Ronnie began, "are given to a senior by his classmates in recognition of a contribution to the school, of participation in school activities or simply in recognition of the senior's unique personality. These are the only awards given strictly to seniors and by seniors, which makes this a really special day for us all. And now—the moment we have all been waiting for—Most Attractive! Linda Sherry!"

The spotlight rested on the sign to the far left. Below the stage, in the audience, Linda let out a shriek and then stumbled up to the stage to stand beside her placard.

Luke stared at the stage in disbelief. The spotlit placard on the stage read simply Linda Sherry.

"Pretty sloppy job they did on the signs, if you ask me," Neil Boggs muttered on Sam's other side.

Sam turned to him indignantly before she remembered that she could hardly defend her handiwork.

She sensed commotion behind her as Caroline Miller, who had overseen the painting of the signs, strained to get a better look. "Somebody's been messing with the signs," Caroline cried. "I tell you they were fine yesterday."

"Most Attractive—" Ronnie boomed up on the stage, "—Cliff Funt." Cliff moved up to claim the male half of the most coveted of the awards, his white teeth flashing in a slightly embarrassed smile.

Her ears made sensitive by guilt, Sam heard Caroline moaning, "But we used the best paint!"

One by one, the chosen seniors, flushed with triumph, mounted the stage. It took quite a while.

Finally, a flourish of trumpets and drums signaled the end of the assembly, and the entire senior class rose and began moving out of the auditorium. Sam let out a sigh of relief. The assembly was over. It had gone off all right, after all.

Luke was still staring at the now-darkened stage, his brow knit in puzzlement. Sam could almost feel his disappointment. Thus would Napoléon have felt, she thought, if Waterloo had been called off because of rain. Luke seemed quite unaware that his certain downfall had been averted. How could he fail to see, Sam thought in exasperation, that this kind of stunt could only lead to his getting thrown off the paper? He seemed to fail to grasp the fundamental law of cause and effect. It was as if he had a blind spot or as if he were programmed to self-destruct.

Later that day at the Wishing Tree, Pip unpacked the special boxed lunch he had brought from home— a fancy salad smelling strongly of goat cheese.

Sam fished a black olive out of the lettuce and nibbled on it while she watched Pip examine his cuticles. "I can't get this paint off," he said. "I've tried it all— fingernail brush, nail file, everything. I feel as if people have been staring at my fingers all day. That's why I decided to bring lunch. I figured I couldn't very well push a cafeteria tray down the line with my hands in my pockets."

"There could be any number of innocent reasons you and I might have white paint on our hands," Sam said airily.

"Don't tell me, let me guess. Last night we worked together on refinishing a fleet of refrigerators."

Sam smiled absently. She speared a bit of tomato drenched in olive oil and looked at it, fascinated by the way the crumbs of cheese clung to the ripe tomato and the way the white cheese echoed the white of the plastic fork. The tomato on the fork had, she decided, a poetic kind of beauty.

Pip had leaned back on his elbows and was staring up at the sky. "This guy, Luke. Did he save your life in the war or something?"

Sam jumped, startled.

"I just don't quite get why you're killing yourself to rescue this fellow, Sam. If you ask me, he'd be the better for a good swift kick in the pants."

"You don't understand him," she said quickly. "He's really a wonderful person, but its like there's a wild joker or something in his deck. I'm not saying I really understand it myself. Sometimes I wonder if it's got something to do with the way his father is always sort of subtly putting him down, and then sometimes I think it's just the star he was born under. I don't know what it is, but he'll be going along fine and then he suddenly breaks out. It's like his sense of humor gets the better of his common sense! I don't think he can help it."

"So you're just being a loyal friend. Is that what you're saying?"

"I wish you could get to know him better," she said earnestly. "I wouldn't be surprised if you two turned out to really like each other."

"I would," Pip snorted.

"Maybe we could all go out for pizza together. We could go to Fino's late tonight, when the place is mobbed."

"If that's what you want to do, it's okay with me."

Sam noticed the lack of enthusiasm in Pip's voice, but she decided to ignore it. She didn't see why Pip couldn't be friends with Luke and Marcy if he just put forth a little effort. No one was easier or more fun than Luke was when he was in a good mood. She had felt the blast of Pip's charm, too, in that smile of his. If each of them could just see the other's best side, she was sure they'd be crazy about each other.

Sam looked at Pip with appraising eyes as she ate the tomato slice. She wondered what she could do to put him in a better humor about Luke before tonight.

"You like the salad?" Pip asked. "It's Greek. My family got hooked on it last summer when we were in Athens."

"It might be better if you don't mention the trip to Greece tonight," Sam said, her eyes fixed anxiously on his. "And, uh, I could give you a ride to Fino's tonight, if you want."

"First of all, Sam, they know I've got a car. Second, your friends didn't like me when they thought I was poor. They aren't going to like me now."

"I think you're taking an unnecessarily pessimistic view of it," said Sam. She hoped she was right about that. She had her fingers crossed.

That night Fino's was a mob scene. The place was full of kids who got off their part-time jobs at nine, and people were spilling out of the packed booths. Waitresses in frilly aprons were weaving their way expertly between the kids, trays balanced on their raised hands.

The beat of the jukebox music throbbed in Sam's head. "There they are," said Sam. She had spotted the pale gleam of Luke's hair across the room.

They made their way over to the booth where Luke was sitting. When they drew closer, they saw Marcy, her short dark hair tucked behind her ears, in the opposite corner. She was checking out kids who passed by, her eyes moving restlessly. The light directly overhead cast shadows under her cheekbones and made her look both older and prettier than usual. Luke was slumped over the table shaking Parmesan cheese out onto its surface. He began tracing patterns in it with his finger.

"Hi, Winston," said Luke, looking up. "Oh, yeah, I guess I'm going to have to call you Byron, now. Byron, a.k.a. Winston. You're a regular roll call of cigarette brands, aren't you?"

"Why don't you just call me Pip?"

Pip sat down next to Marcy, and Sam slid in across from him.

"Have you ordered yet?" asked Sam.

"No, we were waiting," said Luke, "so that we'd be sure to get something that, uh, Pip would enjoy. Right, Marcy?"

Marcy flashed Pip her supersmile, the one with the dimples, and Sam felt relieved to know that Marcy, at least, was willing to make an extra effort to be nice to Pip.

"It's all most of us can do to keep up with one identity," Marcy said. "And now it turns out you had two."

"Not anymore, though," said Pip. "Now just one."

Luke began humming the tune to "Hail, Hail, the Gang's All Here." Sam and Marcy hummed along automatically and slapped their hands down on the table one over the other at the conclusion of the chorus just as they always did.

Belatedly Sam realized that Pip was looking at them as if they were out of their minds. She laughed a little. "We always do that," she said. "I guess it's silly." She had the impulse to kick Luke. He must have realized how their silly little ritual would make Pip feel like an outsider. Even the way he was looking at Pip seemed like a challenge.

Marcy cleared her throat. "So what'd you think of those awards, guys?" she said.

Sam shot her a grateful look. For a brief second there Sam had blanked out and couldn't think of a thing to say to bridge the awkward moment.

"I say Jim Shipman was robbed," Marcy went on. "If he's not Most Attractive, I'm Minnie Mouse. Those eyes, full of scorn, those shoulders. This guy has to be the most attractive."

"If you go for illiterate animals," said Luke.

"Oink," said Marcy, grinning. Then, overcome by a cloud of smoke, she waved her hand in front of her face. "Don't look now," she coughed, "but somebody in the next booth has a pipe."

"You don't smoke, do you?" Luke asked Pip, looking at him through half-closed eyes.

Pip shook his head.

"You just rake in the tobacco profits, huh? Doesn't that bother your conscience a little bit? All those people dying of cancer and emphysema?"

"It's like I read somewhere," Marcy put in. "Every great fortune is founded on a crime."

"It's not Pip's fault his grandfather founded a tobacco company," said Sam in exasperation. "Would you two lay off?"

"I can take care of myself, Sam," said Pip.

"No offense, Pip," said Luke.

"I'm sorry," said Marcy. "I didn't mean anything personal. I just think it's an interesting moral question. I mean, if you just look at it dispassionately, guys, not as if it had to do with Pip personally or anything, you have to ask yourself if somebody inherits money that's kind of tainted, should he refuse to take it? What do you think?"

"I'm having trouble looking at it dispassionately," said Pip. "Somehow, no matter how I turn it, it comes out sounding personal."

"Lets talk about something else," pleaded Sam. "How about that awards assembly? I just hope if I ever get to that point, I can keep my cool better than those kids did today."

"Keeping your cool is not in the best tradition of the Senior Assembly," said Marcy. "Hysteria is essential to the effect."

"I can't kick the feeling something was wrong with that assembly," said Luke, staring down at the spilled Parmesan. "Something seemed out of kilter, not like last year. I can't quite pin it down." He leaned back, his face reflecting genuine puzzlement.

Pip reached over and began tracing a circle in the spilled Parmesan cheese. "Maybe it didn't quite meet your expectations?" he suggested.

Luke was watching Pip's finger in fascination. When he spoke his voice was harsh. "Been doing some painting?"

"Congenital condition," said Pip sadly. "White cuticles run in my family."

Sam blinked rapidly. "I say it's time to order a pizza," she said. "I vote mushrooms. Everybody here like mushrooms? And how about sausage? Everybody like sausage?"

Sam's diversion seemed to work because Pip and Luke backed off a little. But even after the pizza arrived, Sam noticed that Luke could not seem to take his eyes off Pip's fingers.

She knew it was driving Luke crazy trying to figure out exactly what role Pip had played in the ruin of his elaborate joke, but she thought that was good for him. He deserved some punishment after all she and Pip had gone through to save his neck.

Later that night when Sam got home, her mother was sitting in the kitchen drinking a diet cola and leafing through *Beard on Bread*.

"You didn't have to wait up for me, Mom," said Sam.

"I can't help it. I can't sleep until I know you're in," said her mother. "Did you have fun?"

"Not exactly." Sam sat down at the kitchen table and heaved a sigh. "Why can't everybody like each other? Marcy, at least, was making some effort to be nice, but Luke was terrible."

"Don't you think Luke and Marcy might be a little jealous of Pip? The three of you have been friends for so long. A new person undermining that closeness could be threatening."

"I don't know. Everybody's acting so stupid. Even Pip. On the way home tonight he kept saying he doesn't understand why I put up with Luke. He says Luke is unreliable and unrepentant and that if I looked at it closely I'd see that I have nothing in common with him. Nothing in common? What he doesn't understand is that Luke and I have our whole *lives* in common. Why should I have to give all that up?"

"And Luke doesn't like Pip, either, I gather."

"He needles him. He can't let him be. It's 'You don't play football? Oh, too bad,' 'You get your money from tobacco? You must be a moral leper.' Can you think of anything more ridiculous than Luke being holier-than-thou, Mom?"

Her mother smiled. "People can be very difficult," she said.

As the two of them went upstairs to bed, Sam burped. "I think I may be getting an ulcer," she reported gloomily.

"If you get an ulcer at this point, your stomach's going to be Swiss cheese by middle age, Sam, because, believe me, it only gets worse."

"I've got to learn to handle stress," said Sam. "Except that I wouldn't have so much stress to handle if Luke would just behave like a reasonable human being. Why does he have to always get into trouble? Why does he have to be getting his knife into Pip? Why can't we all be friends?" She burped again.

Her mother turned to go into her bedroom. "You might want to mix yourself some bicarb," she said.

Sam did not mix herself any bicarbonate of soda. It was always kept on hand at their house because Sam's father was invariably in need of it when he had bus duty. "An insult," he fumed, "to the professional status of teachers." In Sam's mind, the smell of bicarbonate of soda was associated with defeat, and she was not ready to acknowledge defeat yet.

After she got into her nightgown, she fished her spiral-bound notebook out of her pocketbook and looked at the list of resolutions she had begun so lightheartedly the last week in August.

1. Go steady with Phillip Arrington Byron III**
2. Keep Luke out of trouble!!
3. Be true to myself.
4. Work to overcome prejudices.

Reading between the lines, Sam saw a depressing trend in these resolutions. They had started out bravely and confidently, bristling with asterisks and exclamation points. Now they were winding down to a discouraged whimper of platitudes, as if she no longer had any confidence in making things come out right. It was true, Sam thought miserably—she could feel her confidence ebbing.

What had happened to the Samantha Morrison who secretly felt she had a very good shot at getting Best Personality next year, the serene, friendly girl with two loyal friends and a life full of optimism? That Samantha had become a casualty since Pip had come into her life. If this was love, thought Sam, no wonder they wrote so many sad songs about it.

Chapter Eight

Sunday night, Sam and Pip had driven by Wendy's after the movie to get a late-night snack and were parked at the back of the lot near the dumpster, sharing a large order of fries.

"They don't like me," Pip said. "And I don't see why I should kill myself trying to make them."

Sam's finger touched his cheek. "They just haven't gotten to know you yet," she said.

He kissed her finger. "Well, they've missed their chance," he said. "I'm too smart to go out for pizza with that pair again."

"Marcy was trying to be nice," said Sam.

"What about that crack about 'every great fortune is founded on a crime'?"

"She didn't realize how it was going to sound. Tact isn't her strong point, Pip."

"You can say that again. Okay, I admit I'm not crazy about the idea of Grandfather's money coming from ruining people's lungs. But when it comes right down to it, he didn't hold any gun to peoples' backs to make them buy cigarettes. It was their decision. I'll bet you even if cigarettes were illegal, some people would still be smoking them. Think of the way you see bums picking butts up off the street—there are always going to be guys who would kill for a smoke. And as long as somebody's going to be selling them, why shouldn't it be Byron Tobacco?"

Sam could see flaws in his reasoning. For instance, everything he had said would apply equally well to heroin, and she didn't suppose he would think selling that was okay. She didn't argue with him, though. What was the point? It wasn't as if Pip had the power to close down Byron Tobacco.

"Think of the jobs the company generates," he said. "This city would really hurt if tobacco pulled out. For one thing, the soil around here is so second-rate you can hardly grow anything but tobacco on it anyway." He threw his arm around her. "I can't believe I'm sitting here in the dark with you, talking about the tobacco industry. That's how much that girl got to me."

"Have a french fry," said Sam, consolingly.

Pip did not seem to notice the french fry. "Did you see Luke's face when he saw that paint on my hands? I'll bet he's going crazy trying to figure out how I got on to him. He's probably so paranoid he's having his phone checked right now to see if it's tapped. All that breaking into the school, that mess with the paint—it was worth it to see the look on his face."

Sam sighed and pulled away from him. She could see no sign that the people dearest to her were ready to make an arms agreement.

The next day at newspaper staff, Sam learned that Luke's efforts to write a proper muckraking article had so far met with nothing but frustration. Luke had wrapped up a sample of the cafeteria meat loaf in foil and had transported it to a private laboratory for analysis, but there he had run up against a brick wall. Acme Laboratory had laughed at him.

"We're set up for urinalysis, cholesterol, blood sugar, yes. Meat loaf, no," the lab technician had said. "For all I know, that could be ground pork in there or it could be ground toads. You need a forensic lab."

After this frustrating encounter, Luke was feeling very low. "Look around you," he said as he sat slumped on a table during the meeting. "Incompetence at every level. Half the people alive don't have a clue. If those guys at Acme Lab had an ounce of imagination, a little creativity, I'd be sitting at the typewriter banging out my story this minute."

Sam felt guilty. She had been no help to Luke. Neither had Marcy. The truth was Sam had felt she had had her hands full lately even without trying to help Luke change the direction of the *Traveler*. Being crazy about Pip and getting her homework done was about all she could handle for now.

"In my opinion," said Happy, "some of the people who don't have a clue are right here at this meeting. Who wants to know what's in meat loaf? Nobody."

"Well, for crying out loud, Happy," said Luke. "I keep asking for ideas. If you have a better one, how about telling us, okay?"

"We should to do a series on the arts in Fenterville," she said.

Everyone looked at her in astonishment.

"What arts?" asked Luke blankly. "You going to cover the craft show at the mall?"

"It's a possibility," said Happy, examining her nails.

Luke groaned. "I think you may be just a little confused about what 'art' means, Happy. Handtooled leather wallets are not art. Is this your little joke? Because after my run-in with that lab, I have to tell you I'm not much in a laughing mood. Look, you guys, I'm not giving up. Tomorrow I'm going to go to the back door of the cafeteria and try interviewing the kitchen staff, ask if they'll let me watch them making the stuff. A different approach is all I need. I have to admit, it's taking us a little longer than I thought to get this hard-news segment of the paper going, but we're going to make it yet."

Sam could tell Luke's morale could use a little bit of boosting, so after school when he suggested they drop by the doughnut shop and stuff their faces, she readily agreed, even though she had a ton of stuff to read for American History.

"Do you think Happy was serious about what she said?" he asked her, as soon as the waitress had put the plate of doughnuts in front of them. "I was trying hard not to step on her toes, but I kept having this feeling she was just making fun of me. This is a news story? Heck, the arts in Fenterville isn't news, it's fiction!''

''I don't think you ought to worry about stepping on her toes,'' said Sam. ''Haven't you noticed that everything she says in staff meetings these days is dumb? It's as if she's afraid she might accidentally come out with some idea we could use.''

Luke shrugged his shoulders. ''No use kidding myself about it. She'd love to see me fall on my face. She's not exactly a team player. Good grief, do you hear me? I'm starting to sound like Coach. Who would have guessed it? I tell you, Sam, what I'm finding out is that being editor is a big dose of straight. I go to bed every night thinking about how I have to watch my step. I don't want to make any mistakes. I don't even want Happy to be mad at me. It's not good for the paper. We've got to pull together on this thing because there's no way I can write the entire *Traveler* by myself. I have to admit I didn't realize it was going to be so hard to change the paper's direction. It's like pushing an elephant uphill.''

''It's easier for us all to keep writing the same kind of stuff. And that's not so bad. The *Traveler* has always been a pretty good newspaper. I've never heard any complaints.''

''Not good enough,'' said Luke stubbornly. ''You're right, though. The kids just don't want to change. I can understand it. The *Traveler* has a kind of tradition. I don't want to get people's backs up telling them everything we've been doing up till now stinks. I've just got to keep chipping away at it, and bit by bit the staff will start to see things another way. I think once I show them what a piece of real investigative reporting looks like, they'll get interested in the idea. It's early days to be getting discouraged. We're still working on the first issue after all.''

He dipped his doughnut into his milk and lifted it, dripping, to his mouth.

''Mmmph,'' he said, his mouth full. ''Wanna tell me about Senior Assembly?''

Sam blushed. His question had caught her by surprise. ''We saw you on the roof,'' she admitted. ''And then you drove right past us. We recognized the car.''

''So that's how it happened,'' he said. He put the rest of the doughnut back on the plate and shot a curious look at her. ''We? Who's 'we'?''

''Pip and me. We were walking Fruitcake.''

''I figured that's the 'we' you meant. After I saw that white paint on his fingers, I knew it had to be him. I wish you hadn't gotten him in on this thing, Sam. If you had to mess it up for me, why couldn't you do it by yourself? I hate him knowing all about it. It makes me feel like he's got something on me.''

''I needed his help,'' Sam said indignantly. ''Besides, he was right there with me when I saw you. He saw you, too, Luke.''

''How did you two get in? I went in the air-conditioning vent, but I can't say I'd recommend it. You didn't do that, did you?''

''I was able to pry one of the windows open. We went out by the fire door.''

"There's a fire door?" He grinned. "And all the time I'm scrambling up ladders, practically breaking my neck. I didn't know there was a fire door." He finished off his doughnut, then smiled at her. "Bet old Pip loved that, right? This is a guy who sleeps in ironed pajamas, a guy who brushes his teeth three times a day—I know the type. I can just see him doing a little breaking and entering. I'll bet he had a fit."

"He didn't like it much. But he was willing to help me out."

"You messed up a good joke, Sam."

"No way. Don't you know you left your mark a mile wide on that whole business? You forgot your flashlight, the one with your name on it. Covering up for you, we saved your neck. We kept you from getting kicked off the paper."

"There it goes again," he said sorrowfully. "That 'we' business. Okay, maybe I made a mistake. Maybe I should be thanking you. But don't hold your breath until I thank that Pip guy." He shook his head and looked at Sam. "Marcy's working every day after school now. She's never done that before."

"She's really worrying about getting the money together for college, Luke."

"I know. At least there's no danger of Marcy going away for good. Poor kid. All she's got at home is that run-down apartment, and her mother's either working late or going to those night classes at the college. Heck, you and me are Marcy's family. She needs us. But now you're going off with this guy all the time."

"His name is Pip. Look, just because I'm going out with Pip doesn't mean I've forgotten my old friends."

"I don't like it. Fact is, I don't like *him*."

"I don't want to listen to any more junk about Pip," Sam said firmly. "I want you to lay off him. He's not just any old boy, Luke. This one is different."

"I know," said Luke, suddenly glum. "That's what I don't like about him."

"Look, stupid. I'm here, right? Don't go writing the obituary for the old gang yet."

"Okay," he said, smiling a little. "I'll hold the obit until further notice. I guess it's just—well, you know how it is when you're starting off something new and a little bit scary, something you really care about?"

"Like going off to camp for the first time. Or going off on your first date."

"Yeah, like that. Well, you look around to make sure everything's still the same. You know, that it'll all be there when you need it. Cat still asleep on the windowsill? Check. Favorite pillow still resisting Mom's efforts to pitch it out in the trash? Check. Favorite smooth pebbles still neatly nestled next to the Boy Scout badges?"

"You got Boy Scout badges?"

"Don't spread it around, huh?"

Sam reached for his hand. "We're still here, Luke."

"Better watch it," he said, looking down at their entwined hands. "That Pip guy's going to get jealous."

She punched him. "Idiot!"

Due to the temporary setback in the hard-news story, when the first *Traveler* of the year was put to bed, it was, Sam had to admit, indistinguishable from the twenty or thirty other first issues that had gone before. It had the usual personality profiles, the solid coverage of the football and soccer teams and the latest report on the construction of the new band room. But Luke was obviously going to have to wait a bit longer for a shot at the Pulitzer Prize.

Friday morning the newspaper staff came in before school to get stacks of papers to hand out to the homerooms.

Sam had just dropped off thirty of her papers to Mrs. Pridgeon's room and was staggering on to Mrs. Whitley's room, when she noticed a strange-looking boy at the end of the corridor. He was bald except for a bleached coxcomb of hair sprouting stiffly down the middle of his scalp. He had painted a blue strip between his eyebrows and was dressed in a purple-and-yellow tie-dyed vest and buckskin britches. It wasn't that Sam had never seen a punker before, it was just that she had never known one to get to school early. She wondered what this one was doing down there at the end of the corridor.

After he had moved away, she was curious enough to go over to where he had been standing. There she found a posted sign that said Free Underground Newspapers. Under it, in a cardboard box, was a stack of papers entitled *Cock and Bull*.

Fascinated, Sam picked up a copy. The *Cock and Bull* turned out to be four regular sized sheets of paper stapled together at one corner. It looked to Sam as if it had been printed on a computer. She didn't have time to read it because she had to get her last stack of papers over to Mrs. Whitley's class, but already she had a very bad feeling about it.

After Sam dumped the papers at Mrs. Whitley's room, she had just time enough to run to her own homeroom. When she arrived she saw that a number of people were reading copies of the underground paper.

"I see you've got one, too, Sam," said Tanya Evans. "What do you think of it?"

"I—I don't know," said Sam. "I haven't had a chance to read it yet."

She sank into her desk, and while Mrs. Douglas began passing out the *Traveler*s, she began quickly scanning the *Cock and Bull*. One of the first things to catch her eye was a feature called "Down But Not Out." Sam recognized it right away as an outright parody of one of her favorite features in the *Traveler*, "Up and Away: the Alumni Profile." For this column the *Traveler* interviewed successful alumni and asked how their high-school experiences had helped lead to their present success. Sam had been very proud of the features they had done last year on various successful alums—a trial attorney, a young opera singer and a mother of six who ran a business out of her home. She saw that *Cock and Bull*'s column had rather a different flavor. It was a profile of a guy named Harvey Buller who lived in California on welfare payments. She remembered Harvey Buller because he had been a classmate of her older sister. He was famous for his off-the-wall practical jokes.

It was certainly no surprise to Sam to learn that Harvey Buller was living in a California slum, devot-

ing his life to writing anarchist verse. She only felt
sorry for California. When the bell ending homeroom rang Sam was reading the interview with Harvey
for the second time. It concluded with the zinging line,
"'Hey, man,' Harvey told the *Cock and Bull* in our
telephone interview, 'I owe everything I am today to
good old Lee High.'"

Sam stumbled up from her desk, conscious of a
choking sensation. The depressing thing was, she realized, that the story was fascinating. After all, she
herself had read it twice, though partly, she realized,
that was because the first time she could hardly believe her eyes.

The next period, in algebra class, Sam was aware of
the rustling of pages behind her. She had the unpleasant feeling that everyone at Lee High was avidly reading the *Cock and Bull*.

By the end of the period Sam felt she couldn't stand
it any longer. It was better to know the worst. So when
she got out of algebra, instead of going straight to
newspaper staff, Sam dashed off to the library and
began reading the *Cock and Bull*. She had only been
there a few minutes when Pip came in and found her.

"Have you read it yet?" she asked him in tones of
doom.

"Yup. That Buller character sounds like a candi-
date for a psycho ward to me. Talk about strange."

Sam flipped over a page. "They also have a ten-year
retrospective of what's been happening in heavy-metal
music and a story about sports injuries." The most
disturbing thing about the new paper, she realized, was
that it was interesting. It was as if the dignified *Trav-*

eler had met up with a shady twin who outmatched it on every score.

She remembered what Happy had said about the *Traveler* not being "representative of the writing talents in the school." Could it be that she had been right? Sam never thought she would live to see the day she was saying Happy was perceptive, but Happy had said there was a ground swell of discontent with the *Traveler* and here was the proof of it.

Sam examined the masthead. "*Cock and Bull*," it read. "Published when the spirit moves us. Editor-in-Chief: Jake Furlong." She went rigid. "Look at that," she cried. "Jake Furlong!"

Pip peered over her shoulder. "I see. So what?"

"Jake Furlong is only practically nonverbal, that's what. He's a tackle on the Rebel football team. He spent the entire summer wolfing down Frosties so he could report in to practice at two hundred pounds. I mean, that was his life's ambition. Jake Furlong an editor? Don't make me laugh."

"Shhhhh," said Mrs. Warren, glaring at them.

"He doesn't sound like the editor type," Pip agreed in a whisper.

"He isn't," Sam whispered back. "Another thing—where would he find the time to put out a newspaper with him having to go to football practice every afternoon?"

"I guess he could do it at night."

"No, he's just a figurehead," Sam said slowly. "And I don't have to look far to find out who he's fronting for."

Sam gathered up her books and hurried off to the newspaper staff room. When she walked in nobody commented on her late arrival. In the air of general gloom, no one so much as looked up. Copies of the *Cock and Bull* littered the room. Mr. Perkins had even skipped grading papers in order to sit at his desk reading the new paper.

"Everybody's reading it," said Felicia. "Nobody's even said anything to me about my rundown on the soccer team. And I worked so hard on it, too. I went back three times and checked every single detail."

"Maybe we can get the administration to clamp down on this *Cock and Bull* thing," suggested Reggie. "These people are going all over the school dumping cardboard boxes and paper. That's littering!"

"I already asked at the office," said Marcy. She was doodling on a yellow legal pad. "They got permission."

"Well, they may be able to put out one flashy issue," said Ingrid indignantly, "but getting out an issue every week is something else again."

"Who's bankrolling them?" asked Reggie. "All that paper costs money. I'm with Ingrid. They're not going to be able to keep it up."

Sam noticed that Luke was saying nothing at all. He sat slumped in a desk, lost, evidently, in his own black thoughts.

Sam turned to Happy, who was perched on the edge of a chair, repairing damage to a fingernail with an emery board.

"Happy," she said bluntly, "did you have anything to do with this?"

Everyone turned to look at Happy, who was examining her pink nail with satisfaction. "I did offer a little technical advice to Jake when he asked me," she admitted.

"Consorting with the enemy!" Reggie howled.

"How could you, Happy!" cried Tracy.

"If you had some good ideas, Happy," Luke said mildly, "why didn't you want to bring them in here?"

Happy didn't seem to hear him. Everyone's eyes were on her. Even Mr. Perkins looked up from the paper long enough to give her an odd, speculative look.

"Jake must find it difficult to run a newspaper and go out for football at the same time," Sam said, her eyes narrowed.

"He's been pestering me to take over as editor," Happy said with a sigh. "But I told him my first loyalty is to the *Traveler*."

Reggie made a rude sound.

"Being so close to the editor of the *Cock and Bull* as you are," Sam said sarcastically, "maybe you have some idea what his plans for the future are?"

Happy spread her fingers wide apart and smiled. "I guess he'll just continue offering the *Cock and Bull* as a haven for the brilliant, disaffected elements of this school of ours. That's only a wild guess."

"I don't see any reason to panic, people," said Marcy. "With no classtime to work on their paper, no funding and no—" she looked pointedly at Happy

"—real leadership, these *Cock and Bull* people may find it pretty hard to keep up their standard."

Sam appreciated Marcy's attempt to cheer everybody up, but she could not take much comfort in what she said. If Happy was behind the *Cock and Bull*, it wasn't likely it would fold any time soon. Even Happy's worst enemy couldn't accuse her of giving up easily. It was pretty obvious now why everything she had said during staff meetings was so lame. She didn't want to help out at all at the *Traveler*. If she couldn't be on top, she refused to play. She had founded a whole new newspaper rather than help Luke.

After school Sam waited at Luke's locker. He had been uncharacteristically silent during newspaper staff, and Sam had the strong feeling it would be better for him not to be alone this afternoon.

"Hi," he said, throwing his books into his locker with a thump.

"It's starting to smell in there," offered Sam. "Maybe you ought to take your gym socks home."

"Get off my case, Sam."

"Sorry. I just came by to see if you wanted to go get some ice cream or something with me. What do you say?"

"Okay," he said listlessly.

"You'll have to drive. My car's still in the shop."

When they left school they drove in the direction of Wendy's, but as they passed K mart, Luke spotted a sign on the store marquee that said Banana Splits— Buy One, Get One Free. Without saying anything, he abruptly turned into the huge K mart parking lot.

He parked the car, threw the door open, and not looking behind him, charged on into the store. Sam had to run to keep up with him. She followed him past island after island of merchandise—a cookie-sheet special, a display of cheap cuckoo clocks, a forest of ties and belts, an Aladdin's cave of costume jewelry—to the snack bar at the rear of the store.

"Two banana splits," Luke told the woman at the soda fountain. "Extra whipped cream on mine."

Sam was encouraged by his asking for extra whipped cream. That had to mean his will to live was not completely gone.

The woman in the white apron squirted some whipped cream on top of the ice cream and carefully balanced a half a maraschino cherry on top. She shoved the two splits toward Sam and Luke.

"My treat," Sam insisted. She laid the money on the counter.

They took their glass boats of ice cream to a booth near a carousel of gray sweat suits. A booming voice echoed over their heads, "Attention, K mart shoppers...." Sam could hear a child crying somewhere over in sportswear.

Finally Luke spoke. "That blinking *Cock and Bull*'s so good," he said, digging his spoon into the ice cream with unnecessary force. "That's what I can't get away from. I might as well just hang it up."

"Hang it up?" Sam wailed in dismay. "We have just begun to fight!"

"I don't think so, Sam. I gave it my best shot, and it wasn't good enough. I hate to have to sit here and tell you that Happy is a better editor than me, but there's no sense kidding myself."

"Do you think she wrote that entire newspaper? You know she didn't, Luke. She's got her hands on some people who can write and who have a sort of different point of view. She's put together a good, strong, offbeat staff, that's all. You're working with reporters who're bogged down in their old ways. Happy was able to go out and start fresh. Don't you see that part of the appeal of the paper is its shock value?"

"I don't know. You know what I feel like?" he said. "I feel numb. What about my dreams of being a big-time newspaper reporter? It's pretty obvious I just can't cut it. You know what my dad said when I told him I got editor? 'That's fine, Luke, but just remember all those C's in English and keep in mind that you just may not be quite the hotshot you think you are.' I guess he's right. I don't feel like such a hotshot right now."

"But you got C's in English because you only did half the work, not because you aren't any good at it."

"Maybe I ought to just turn in my resignation now and let Happy take over."

"No!"

Luke looked down at his melting ice cream. "You think I'll feel better about this tomorrow?"

"Golly, you're bound to."

"Right," he said ironically. "How could I feel worse?"

"Promise me you won't do anything rash," she pleaded. "Aren't you willing to fight for the paper?"

"I don't know. Maybe. I'll have to see how I feel."

"Promise me you won't resign this week anyway, okay?"

"I just can't stand that smug smile on Happy's face. She's just sitting there thinking, 'You just can't cut it.'"

"What good will it do to quit?"

"I won't have to watch her laugh in my face, that's what good it'll do."

"Promise me you won't resign tomorrow, okay?"

"All right, Sam. I guess I can stand another day of it. I guess I can put up with anything for one day."

"What did Marcy have to say about this? Have you had a chance to talk to her?"

Luke smiled. "You know Marcy," he said. "She said she wanted to remind me of the philosopher's immortal words, 'What does not destroy me, makes me stronger.'"

"Golly, you'd think she could come up with something more cheerful than that," said Sam, disgusted.

"Well, she'd just been by the office talking to Mr. Hendley, trying to find some way to stop the thing. She couldn't get anywhere with him. I think she's pretty down herself."

As they were leaving the store, they again passed by the men's ties, and Luke paused there. He took a tie from the rack, looped it around his neck and, standing in front of the round mirror on the counter, tied it on and adjusted it carefully. Then he began walking out of the store.

Sam, frozen in her steps, felt her face go hot and cold at the same time as she realized Luke had no intention of paying for the tie. It was like a nightmare, one of those awful dreams where something terrible is happening and you can't stop it because your feet won't move. When Luke walked out the big glass doors Sam held her breath in every expectation that a store detective would grab him by the collar, but nothing happened. Nothing at all.

Sam, wooden with embarrassment, finally followed him out of the store. When she got to the car, Luke was standing by it waiting for her. She looked at him, unable to speak. How she wished he were a little kid so she could march him back into the store to return the tie and apologize, the way her parents had marched her in to return the pack of gum she had forgotten to pay for when she was four.

Luke casually pulled the tie off and let it dangle from his hand. Sam found herself staring at it, mesmerized. "I don't know what I'm going to do about the paper," he said. "I guess I'll stay in there slugging a little bit longer."

He stepped over to a nearby Volkswagen, and his back to Sam, fiddled with its antenna. Sam winced. She hoped he wasn't going to steal the VW's antenna. She didn't know what she would do if he snapped it off, but she suspected she would faint. She was already feeling strangely woozy. When he stepped away from the car, Sam darted a glance toward the antenna and was relieved to see it was still there. The tie, however, was in a bow at the top of it. Luke smiled at her. He had never looked more angelic, with his disordered white-gold locks and his guileless blue eyes.

When he was driving her home, Sam found she could not make herself say anything to him about what had happened. She just didn't have it in her to confront him. And the only way she could go on approximating a normal person was to try to pretend that what had happened hadn't really happened.

Luke dropped her off in front of her house, and she stood there on the sidewalk and watched his car as it turned the corner and then disappeared.

Chapter Nine

By the time Sam got up to her room, she had re-covered enough from her experience to try to make sense out of it. When she began sorting it out in her mind, she decided she had gotten a glimpse of some-thing disturbing but significant. Luke had been run-ning when he went into the store, as if invisible monsters had been at his heels. And then, when she thought about it, hadn't there been something almost ceremoniously defiant in the way he had knotted that tie on the antenna? Was the shoplifting, she won-dered, some kind of ritual to banish whatever it was that was after him?

In the past when Luke had rocketed out of bounds, she had always thought he was thumbing his nose at other people—at society, at the establishment, at people taller than he was. She had never realized that he might be thumbing his nose at his own fears.

Sam would have loved to talk over her ideas about Luke with her mother, because when it came to getting inside people's minds, her mother was one of the world's best. She couldn't bring herself to tell her mother about the shoplifting episode, though, because even though it had been Luke who had stolen the tie, Sam felt like an accomplice. Her parents would say she should have stopped Luke from leaving the store, that she should have reminded him firmly that he needed to pay for the tie. At the very least, when they got out to the car she should have insisted that he return it. She knew what she should have done. But knowing it and doing it were two different things. She had discovered that it wasn't easy to cover up for Luke time after time and then suddenly turn and accuse him. It wasn't only that she disliked confrontation, she had settled into a pattern with Luke, almost an unspoken conspiracy, to ignore and cover up his occasional rule breaking. It was as if she were under a spell that commanded her to go on acting the way she always had before. For the first time she began to think that maybe Pip had been right and she had been wrong. When Luke sabotaged the Senior Assembly, she should have stayed out of it and let him live with the consequences of his actions.

But the problem, she thought glumly, was that one of the consequences of Luke being in trouble was that Happy would inevitably get to be editor. Sam knew that it had been for her own purely selfish reasons that she had let herself be led into this sticky situation.

As soon as Sam judged Marcy would be in from work, she dialed her number.

"Hullo," said Marcy. "Marcy is not at home. This is her answering machine. She is in the bathroom crying her heart out."

"Oh, come on, Marce. It's not that bad."

"It's awfully close," Marcy said. "Did you see Luke's face? He looked like death. Did you notice how he didn't say anything all the rest of the day?"

"I treated him to a banana split after school. I didn't think he ought to be left alone."

"That was such a good idea, Sam," Marcy said warmly. "I was wishing I could do the same thing, but I had to rush off to my job, as usual."

"He's really upset," Sam said. When she thought about the tie festooning the Volkswagen's antenna, she had a vision of prison doors opening up to receive Luke, complete with barred windows and yellow-toothed murderers getting ready to jump him when he came through. Involuntarily, she shivered.

"I know that Luke's upset," Marcy said. "I was just telling you that. I don't feel exactly great myself."

But you don't know quite how upset he is, thought Sam gloomily, and Sam didn't like to tell her. Cynical as Marcy was, Sam couldn't remember her saying anything critical of Luke. How could Sam bear to tarnish Luke in Marcy's eyes by telling her about the shoplifting incident?

"Do I dare to hope you are calling to confide in me your fantastic plan to overturn the *Cock and Bull*?" Marcy asked.

"Not exactly."

"I was afraid of that. It's awful, isn't it? You know what really gets to me the most, Sam? Now that we've seen just what Happy's up to, I know we haven't seen the worst of it. It's obvious what's going to happen next."

"It is?" said Sam. "I mean, she's already done it, hasn't she? What else can she do?"

"Next she's going to validate that paper, that's what. Instead of being an underground paper, it'll be a regular school publication. I can hear her now in that phony voice of hers telling Mr. Hendley, 'Lee needs an alternative newspaper.' She'll request a faculty adviser, then she'll petition the Student Council for a share of the activity fee."

"But the Student Council's already portioned out the activity fee. There's no more money left."

"She'll want half of the *Traveler*'s money, naturally."

"She can't have it!" Sam yelped. "Look, how can you possibly know what Happy's going to do?"

"It's the smart thing to do. It's what I would do myself if I were in her position. Ergo, that's what she'll do. Just watch. Betcha. You see, that would put her in a terrific position. Once she gets half the activity money, Luke will have to preside over a diminished little paper. It will have maybe one page, no pictures. He may get depressed enough to leave. Why do I say 'may'? He's already depressed enough to leave. Then Happy could take over the *Traveler* as editor, fold the *Cock and Bull* and return the *Traveler* to its former glory with its full share of the activity fee. On the other hand, if Luke hangs on in spite of everything, Happy can simply go over to the *Cock and Bull* and be editor there, a big frog in that little puddle. Either way, she's better off than she is now. You have to give her credit. The girl is no slouch."

Sam did not feel she had to give Happy credit, and while breath remained in her body she would refuse to do so. "I never thought of any of that," she said, suddenly even more depressed. "That's awful. What can we do?"

"I was hoping you'd have some ideas."

"If only troubles would just come one at a time instead of sort of washing over you like a tidal wave, I could cope better," Sam said desperately. "Marce, why doesn't Luke like Pip?"

"I think you're going round the bend, Sam. What does that have to do with anything? Who cares? We're fighting for the survival of the *Traveler* here."

"I care. I feel as if I could stand it all better if we were all together the way we used to be. Luke hasn't said anything to you about Pip?"

"No. But you must have noticed that tall, conceited types driving expensive cars and living in prestige neighborhoods do not always draw unmixed admiration."

"Pip isn't conceited. He's sweet."

"I'm not saying it's Pip's fault, Sam, but it sticks out all over him that he doesn't give a flip about what other people think, that he figures he's above the rules that apply to everybody else. It's in his eyes, even in the way he holds himself. I guess that's what money does to people. You would have noticed it yourself if you hadn't met him when he was dripping with mud. I doubt that even Pip could pull off looking rich when he was covered with mud.''

"He's not stuck-up at all," protested Sam. "He's only a little shy. You're all wrong about him, Marce. And I think Luke and Pip might really like each other if they got to know each other better."

"Look, Sam, don't you think you'd better give up this absurd fantasy about the lion lying down with the lamb and concentrate on fielding Happy's next move?"

Sam swallowed all the retorts that sprang to her lips. Marcy was right. This was a crisis. She was going to have to concentrate on the issue at hand. "I'll try to think of something," she said.

"Good."

After Sam hung up, she sat in her room staring at her copy of the *Cock and Bull* and thinking about what she could have said to Marcy. It wasn't Pip who didn't give a flip what people thought about him, it was Marcy. And as for thinking he was above the rules, that was Luke, not Pip. Sam wished she had pointed these things out to Marcy. The problem with that was that Marcy was really making an effort to be fair about Pip, and Sam knew that attacking her wasn't going to help improve her attitude any.

Sam heaved a sigh. She felt a little uncomfortable when she realized this was the second time in one day she had avoided telling her friends what she thought. Quite possibly, she had no moral courage whatever. On the other hand, she thought a little bitterly, it was highly doubtful that a brutally frank sort of person could have stayed friends all these years with Marcy and Luke. It disturbed her to find herself having these disloyal feelings. She had never sat around finding fault with Marcy and Luke before. Why couldn't they be friends in the simple old unquestioning way they had always been? What had happened to the three musketeers, the kids who were going to be friends forever?

Staring at the underground paper, Sam forced herself to concentrate on the problem at hand. After all, if Happy got to be editor, she was going to have even more problems to deal with. The first order of business was to save the *Traveler*. She stared at the newspaper until her head began to hurt. Was there any trace of criminal libel, that dread of Mr. Perkins? Sam knew that if the *Cock and Bull* stepped out of line on that, the principal would be quick to pull in those cardboard boxes and rip down those signs saying Free Underground Newspapers. But as she examined the paper closely, she was forced to admit that though the copy was daring, unfortunately, none of it looked libelous.

Next she studied the bylines, trying hard to conjure up faces to go with the names. She didn't remember running into any of these people. Where had they been hiding? She got out her yearbook and looked them up. Three of them she didn't find at all, which suggested that either they had just moved to Fenterville or they were sophomores. She did, however, find Richard Evans, Kilroy Cutchin and Anita Jolley.

Richard Evans, the author of the heavy-metal article, was a slender black boy who had been, according to the yearbook, a sophomore last year. Sam could hardly believe this boy was actually in her own class. Maybe it was a typographical error. She could have sworn she had never seen that owlish stare before. Yet there was his picture in the annual, proof positive that he had at least attended Lee. She would have to ask Reggie about him.

Kilroy Cutchin, who had done the *Cock and Bull* story on sports injuries, looked out from his sophomore picture with a blank open-mouthed stare. His hair fell in a limp bang over his forehead, and he appeared to be wearing a sweatshirt. It was with a shock that Sam recognized the features of the punk kid who had been putting out the newspapers that morning. Kilroy had evidently undergone a remarkable transformation over the summer. It was amazing how different a person could look with the hair stripped off his scalp and blue war paint on his face.

Anita Jolley was fat. At first that was all Sam could take in about the girl who had done *Cock and Bull*'s profile of Harvey Buller. She saw the roundness of Anita's nose and jowls, the telltale bulge under her chin. But having read the Harvey Buller article, Sam had a certain respect for Anita Jolley already. Underneath those folds of flesh was evidently a steel-trap mind and a perverse sense of humor.

These people *are* the paper, Sam told herself. Happy is only using them. There must be some way to get to them, to reason with them, to bribe them. There must be something they want, some plea they would listen to. But even as she was staring at their pictures, Sam had the queasy feeling that these kids were beyond her reach.

What struck her was that she had never seen three faces that were, from a social point of view, more doomed. Sam did not normally dwell on the misfortunes of people who were out of it. She preferred not to think much about social disaster, just as she preferred to avoid those newspaper stories about starving people in India. But scrutinizing the faces of Richard, Kilroy and Anita, she recognized at once that these were people without niches. She was certain of that. It was as if *loser* had been branded on their foreheads.

And something told her these kids would not give her the time of day. For them, Sam Morrison with her secure spot on Student Council, her slot on the *Traveler* and her reasonably attractive body, was the moral equivalent of those people who wore pounds and pounds of diamonds during the Great Depression. These kids would hate her, she just knew it. And though she did not like to admit it, Sam knew that she was not a person who stood up well to being hated. Above all she liked to be liked. She would wilt before their hostile eyes. If somebody was going to approach them, she was not the person.

Marcy would have been better, Sam thought. Marcy was a fighter. She got too mad to worry about what people were thinking of her. Sam would have unhesitatingly picked up the phone and appealed to Marcy to go as an ambassador to those people if she hadn't been aware that Marcy was kind of short of tact. Look at how she had got Pip's back up. She was no negoti-

ator. And if she made them mad, that could be fatal.
All hope of compromise would be at an end. No, she
couldn't risk sending Marcy.

Sam went to bed that night no closer to a solution
to her myriad problems than she had been before.

When Sam got to school the next morning, she
spotted a notice posted outside the school office.

Meeting of the *Cock and Bull* Staff!

Come one, come all. If you can write and have
something to say, the *Cock and Bull* needs YOU.
At this meeting we will discuss plans for EX-
PANSION. Come to Room 206 after school and
have a voice in the future. The *Cock and Bull* is
an equal-opportunity employer.

Sam's books almost slipped out of her grasp. Under the circumstances, the word *expansion* had a sin-
ister sound.

For a second she had the impulse to reach up and rip
the notice off, but then she realized that it was to her
advantage that the *Cock and Bull* be meeting where it
could be watched. If only someone from the *Traveler*
could go to the meeting and find out exactly what they
planned to do next! Better yet would be to send some
smooth-tongued person who could keep them from
actually doing it.

Sam walked to her homeroom in a daze. On further reflection, she had decided that it would not do at
all for a member of the *Traveler*'s staff to go to that
meeting. It was too obvious that staff members had a
vested interest in destroying the *Cock and Bull*. What

was needed was some attractive, tactful person whom they could trust absolutely, but who had no official connection with the *Traveler*, someone who could pose as a prospective staffer and in a subtle way make the *Cock and Bull* staff stop publishing their dumb paper.

During homeroom Sam took out her spiral-bound notebook and made a list of the qualities needed by the person who was to infiltrate the *Cock and Bull* staff meeting.

1. attractive
2. tactful
3. trustworthy
4. no official ties to the *Traveler*.

At the bottom of the page, she wrote in block letters "PIP!" She smiled at the page a moment, congratulating herself. She had come up with the perfect person.

At newspaper staff, Sam was careful not to mention her plan to get Pip to infiltrate *Cock and Bull*'s meeting. She did not want to tip her hand to Happy.

She did, however, show the other kids the list she had compiled of *Cock and Bull* staff members. "Does anybody know any of these kids?" she asked. "Does anybody have any special rapport with them?"

Happy peeked over Sam's shoulder at the list. "I know them all—very slightly, you understand. And my impression is that they are all kids of unimpeachable integrity who simply can't be bought." She smiled sweetly at Sam.

"Nobody's asking you, Happy," said Sam, glaring back at her. She turned to Reggie. "What about this guy, Richard Evans, Reggie? He's black. Don't you know him?"

Reggie looked at the name. "Ain't no such dude."

"Well, he's in the yearbook."

"Misprint," said Reggie positively. "Somebody made him up. You know me, Sam, I know everybody. I get around. I've never, but never, seen any Richard Evans."

"He could call himself Rick, Ricky, Dick, Dickie, maybe he goes by his initials or uses a nickname."

Reggie shrugged. "I'll ask around, but I don't think so."

"What are you going to say to these guys if you do find somebody who has so-called 'rapport' with them?" Luke asked.

"I don't know exactly," said Sam. "I just feel like there ought to be a way to negotiate with them. We could find out their goals, make some sort of compromise."

Luke shrugged. "Good luck," he said.

A pall seemed to settle over the newspaper staff for the rest of the period.

At lunch Sam sat cross-legged on the grass waiting for Pip. When she saw his tall figure striding toward her, the sun gleaming on his dark hair, she could feel her pulse quickening with pleasure. "Pip!" she cried. "Am I glad to see you!"

He raised his eyebrows a little but looked pleased. He sat down and began unwrapping a sandwich. "I don't know what it is," he said, "but ever since you told me about Luke taking that meat loaf to the lab, I'm sort of turned off of the cafeteria. You haven't touched your food, Sam. Don't you ever eat?"

"Not now. I've got too much on my mind. Can you help me out?"

Pip's hand, in the process of conveying the sandwich to his mouth, paused in midair.

"It's this underground newspaper. I need someone to go to their meeting so I can find out exactly what they're up to next."

"In other words, you need a spy?"

"Well, if you want to put it in that crass way, yes. But also, I need a sort of an agent, a diplomat, someone who can persuade them not to do whatever it is they plan to do."

"I don't see why you're so excited about this underground paper."

"Marcy thinks they're going to move to take away part of the *Traveler*'s share of the student activity fee! We might have to cut the size of the paper, cut out the pictures. It would be a disaster!"

"I didn't know you cared that much about the paper. A smaller paper means less work. That way everybody's happy."

"I do care about the paper! I don't want to see it shrink down to a page of administration announcements. Besides, Luke is already so upset—"

"Now we come to it."

"What do you mean by that?" asked Sam, taken aback by the set expression on his face.

"Sam, I'm not going to go spy for Luke. You shouldn't even be asking me to."

"But if I go myself, they're going to see right away that I'm from the *Traveler*. It has to be somebody with no official ties to the paper."

"Everybody knows I go out with you."

"But these kids aren't going to know that. From what I can tell, they are really out of it. They aren't going to be on the grapevine. As far as they're concerned you're a civilian, no ties to the rival paper at all."

"What about you?"

"What do you mean? I just told you they'll know I'm on the paper. For one thing, Happy might be there and—"

"I mean, as far as you're concerned, are we going together?"

Sam looked at him blankly. "Of course."

"Then how come it's always Luke this, Luke that, Sam? I'm beginning to wonder whether it's Luke you want instead of me. I'm always hearing girls talk about how good-looking he is, and when I stop and think about it, it seems he's pretty much the center of your life."

"He's an old friend," Sam said, recoiling. "I don't think of Luke that way at all."

"It seems to me like you're thinking of him morning, noon and night."

"No," Sam said. "You're wrong."

"Okay, I'm wrong. I'm also not going to any *Cock and Bull* meeting."

"Okay," said Sam.

"So this time we just let Luke sink or swim? I mean, this time, Sam, it's him or me."

Sam could feel anger rising within her at that ulti-
matum. There was no reason at all why she should
have to give up her friends for him, any more than she
should have to give up him just because her friends
didn't like him. But more important than her anger
right now was the fear of losing Pip. She had made a
serious misstep, taking his good-natured help for
granted. Now she might be losing him.

"You've got the wrong idea, Pip. You really do."

"So we let this guy save himself for a change?"

Sam swallowed. "Actually, I've been thinking
maybe you were right about that. Something happened that made me think that maybe I shouldn't have
been covering up for Luke. I guess it was, in some
ways, a bad idea."

Pip shot her an acute look. "Now he's getting into
big-time trouble, huh? What's he been up to?"

"Nothing big."

"Still covering up for him?"

Sam flushed. "Okay, I can't seem to help covering
up for him," she said. "It's, like, a habit at this point.
He's a friend of mine. But that's all."

He smiled at her, and she was relieved to see that the
smile reached his eyes. "We're going to talk about
something besides Luke, now? For a change?"

"Okay."

He moved closer to her and put his arm around her.
"Hey, I can feel your ribs. Eat something!"

Sam picked up her sandwich and resolutely bit into
it. Her mouth was dry, the sandwich tasted like saw-
dust, and all she could think about was Luke and

Happy, and losing Pip, and the dumb *Cock and Bull*.
Bon appétit! she thought bitterly.

"That's better," said Pip. "Here, try a bite of mine.
I use lots of fattening mayonnaise."

Sam took a bite of Pip's sandwich, too. It had lots
of mayonnaise. She had never been fond of mayonnaise. Sam had decided she would have to go to the
Cock and Bull meeting herself. She would wear sunglasses as a disguise. Pip didn't have to know about it.

Chapter Ten

That afternoon after school Sam went in the girls' room and put on her rose-colored sunglasses. She still looked indisputably like Sam Morrison. Then she spotted a wet rubber band lying on the sink and scooped it up. Pulling a handful of her hair up over her head, she secured it with the rubber band and dribbled a little water on her bangs. Next she took her gym socks out of her gym bag and put them on. Sam glanced in the mirror and shuddered. She should fit right into the *Cock and Bull* meeting. She only hoped she wouldn't run into anybody she knew on the way to Room 206.

Sam peeked cautiously out the girls' room door. No one was in the hall outside. School had been out for five minutes, and the building must be almost empty by now. She threw her shoulders back, and with what bravery she could muster, headed toward the stairs.

Sam found herself forcibly reminded of those adventure movies where the heroine got thrown into a pit of snakes where only her handy lasso could save her. That was the way she felt, only she didn't have a lasso.

She was afraid of meeting all those *Cock and Bull* writers face-to-face. She knew they would despise her. And she did not even have the advantage of being armed with indignation. What had those guys ever done except write a more interesting paper?

She wondered if Happy was going to be there. If so, did Happy wear a nerd disguise to these meetings, too? It was hard to imagine. Happy was the sort of person the bumper sticker Born to Shop was created for.

Sam approached Room 206 with faltering steps. A boy who looked like a direct descendant of Attila the Hun was going in the room just ahead of her. He wore boots, a wide black belt studded with brass that must have made it impossible for him to bend over, and no shirt at all. He looked as if he oiled his chest.

Sam forced herself to go inside. She sat down in the desk nearest the door because her knees felt weak. Unfortunately that happened to be the desk right next to Attila the Hun. Sam smiled at him uncertainly. His beady eyes rested on her. Still looking at her, with great deliberation, he cracked his knuckles.

Jake Furlong was sitting at the front desk fidgeting. Jake, with his massive build, always looked slightly out of place in a classroom, but today he looked as if he was having to force himself not to bolt.

Sam noticed he had what looked like a prepared script laid before him.

Looking around the room, Sam spotted Kilroy Cutchin right away. No one else was wearing blue paint between his eyebrows. Today he also wore red platform shoes with plaid shoelaces, so it was possible, at least, that he had a sense of humor.

Anita Jolley had taken a seat near the front. Her face looked a little squashed together, as if someone had sat on her head. Her hips bulged out the sides of the desk, and it looked as if she had not washed her hair lately, but to Sam she seemed to radiate confidence.

There were several other kids there as well, sophomores presumably, but there was no sign of Richard Evans.

"I got to make this short, guys," said Jake, "because I gotta run to practice." He picked up the script and began reading it, pausing slightly after each word.

"Welcome to the second meeting of the *Cock and Bull*, the equal opportunity newspaper. Our first edition was a fantastic success, as you all know, and we now plan to move to leg—" he hesitated, then went on more confidently "—leg-itimize our paper. Next week we will apply for a faculty adviser and—"

"I don't know," said Anita. "I figure we don't need a faculty adviser telling us what to do. We're better off as an underground paper."

Jake cast a desperate look down at his script as if hoping it would provide a way to cope with this sudden independence of mind in his staffers.

"We've got to be practical about this," Kilroy put in. "Paper costs money. Where we going to get money?"

"Bank robbery?" suggested Anita, her eyes glittering. Sam could not tell whether she was kidding or not.

"Listen, you guys," said Jake. "I gotta go to practice. Can I just get on with this? Next week we're going to put in for a faculty adviser and a share of the activity money. We're going to make an official motion before the Student Council—"

"Is this an dictatorship?" said Anita. "Or a democracy? We've got to have a full and intelligent debate of this issue. What I think we'd better do is begin by everybody's introducing themselves. We've got some new faces here today, I can see," she said, staring at Sam.

Sam could feel herself going red. Any moment she would be exposed as a spy. What could have been in her mind to think about coming to this meeting? Not only was she afraid of Anita Jolley, she had this creepy feeling that whatever was wrong with all the people in this room might be catching.

"Like I was saying, I gotta get to practice—" Jake said weakly.

"We've got to ask ourselves where we're going," said Anita. "If this is a real underground paper offering a genuine alternative to the dreck they dish out at the *Traveler*, maybe a faculty adviser isn't what we need."

"But if we were official," Kilroy pointed out, "we could work on the paper during our study hall."

"That's just what I was trying to tell you," said Jake, eyeing the door with longing. Sam supposed he was figuring out how many laps the coach would make him run for being this late.

"The question is," said a serious-looking oriental boy, "whether this paper or any paper can long endure as an underground entity or whether we must risk losing our identity in order to save ourselves."

Sam noticed Anita Jolley looking at her in a way that made her want to rip the rubber band out of her hair and run for the exit.

Just then she heard a familiar shuffling sound behind her and wheeled around in the desk. Everyone else had turned around, too.

"Hi, Jake," said Luke. "Can I come in?"

Jake looked down at his script, then tossed it aside in despair. "I guess so. The fact is, Luke, I've just plain got to get to practice. You wouldn't want to read this stuff for me, would you?"

"Nah," said Luke. "But I would like to say a few words on my own."

All eyes were on him. There was a distinct advantage, Sam realized, in being as good-looking as Luke was. Good-looking was a kind of enchantment for the eyes. Even Anita Jolley's face had taken on a new softness looking at Luke.

Luke sat on Jake's desk and regarded them with blue eyes filled with infinite charity. "I just want to say how much I admire the work you've done on the *Cock and Bull*," he said. "It's a paper with punch and excitement. Personally, I'd be proud to be associated with it, and that's why I'm hoping you'll listen to my proposition today. I'd like to ask you all to come aboard the *Traveler*, be on the regular staff."

"We want our independence," glowered Kilroy. "You can't buy us."

Luke looked at Kilroy quizzically. "I'm not Simon Legree," he said. "Ask anybody. We run a loose ship. You can be like a paper inside a paper. I've talked to Mr. Perkins and Mr. Hendley about this, and they've said I can make you the offer. No writing samples, no competition—you get automatic entry onto the *Traveler*. That means everybody who has already published in this last issue of the *Cock and Bull*."

"I don't think it's such a good idea," said Jake uneasily.

"Yo! Go with that, Jake!" said Luke, grinning. "I'm not twisting anybody's arm. Whoever's interested, just show up at the newspaper room second period tomorrow. We can get your schedules rearranged, but we've got to know tomorrow, before the end of the drop-and-add period."

As soon as Luke stopped speaking, the meeting fell into total disorder. Kilroy and Anita were engaged in a heated argument.

With an anxious look around, Jake gathered up his script and quietly slipped out. Whatever he had promised Happy, he could no longer resist the siren call of football practice. Sam decided it was time for her to leave, too. As she made her way as inconspicuously as possible out the door, she spotted a black kid slithering stealthily out behind her. When she turned and stared at him, he made a sharp right turn and headed in the opposite direction. Richard Evans did exist after all.

As soon as Sam got clear of the building, she tore the rubber band out of her hair, then broke loose and ran. She was too exuberantly happy to walk in the usual way. As she careered around the administration building, she saw that the junior–senior parking lot was almost empty, but next to her own old blue Plymouth she saw Pip sitting in his white Mercedes.

It was almost too good to be true, Sam thought. It was like the maraschino cherry on the whipped cream, finding him there. "Pip!" she yelled. She ran over to the white car, flung its door open and threw herself in on the seat beside him. "Kees me, keed," she cried. "I'm so happy!"

He grinned, put his hands on her shoulders and pressed her against the seat and kissed her for a long time.

Sam was distinctly short of breath when he drew away, but she felt wonderful, as if her head were floating.

"I'm so glad to see you!" she said.

"Good. Do you want to tell me what we're celebrating?"

"Luke has saved the newspaper!"

"Oh." He did not seem particularly pleased.

Sam looked at him, a puzzled frown growing between her brows. "But why were you waiting for me? You've been hanging around here a pretty long time."

"Yup." He glanced over to the other side of the lot where Luke's green Pontiac was still parked. "In fact, I was beginning to wonder where you were."

"I decided to be the spy at the meeting myself," she explained. "I just couldn't stand the suspense, wondering what they were up to, wondering what disaster was going to come down next. So I just went. It was awful. I mean, I was really scared. You should have seen the way that Anita Jolley looked at me. I sort of identified with Miss Muffet in a way I never had before. You know, that part where the spider sat right down beside her? A very bad scene, I promise you. I was sure that any minute she was going to unmask me as an agent of the *Traveler* and then, whammy, it'd be the kiss of the spider woman or something equally bad. It came to me suddenly that I was simply not cut out at all to be a spy.

"But then suddenly in came Luke! Like the cavalry to the rescue, except without the horses. He was great! I would never have thought he had it in him. He didn't talk it over with me or Marcy or anybody. I don't know how he thought of it. But he must have figured out what to do and then checked it out with Mr. Perkins and Mr. Hendley to get their okay before he came to the meeting. Imagine! Luke checking with the people in charge! Imagine Luke actually thinking ahead! It boggles the mind. It just goes to show what people can do when something is important enough to them.

"He came right into that meeting and invited all those kids to join the staff of the *Traveler*. How about that! He had them in the palm of his hand. Not all of them agreed, but it was pretty obvious to me that the offer was tempting to some of them. They started fighting about it right away. I'm sure at least some of them are going to take the bait. Maybe even all of them. You could kiss me again, if you want.''

Pip pulled her close to him, a maneuver that took some agility in the cramped quarters of the car, and began kissing her. Sam could feel all her troubles evaporating. Everything was going to work out somehow. She just knew it. Pip and Luke and Marcy would become friends. The *Traveler* would win the Pulitzer Prize. She would grow two inches. Fruity would lose five pounds. Pip would love her forever.

She and Pip occupied themselves quite happily, kissing for some minutes before Sam began to have the uncomfortable feeling that she was being watched. She peeked around behind her. One row over Anita Jolley was getting into a Volkswagen that had been painted with dull black house paint.

Sam groaned. "Anita Jolley sees me making out in a Mercedes. Something tells me she's not going to like that."

"Who is Anita Jolley, and who cares what she likes?" said Pip, nibbling on her ear.

"She's one of the writers on the *Cock and Bull*. That means she's probably going to be on the *Traveler* now," said Sam. The implications of that were only just now slowly beginning to hit her. She began to wonder if her celebration had been just a little premature.

"That's good," he murmured.

"I guess so. I mean, sure it's good," she said uncertainly.

Kilroy Cutchin's shoes made a clacking sound on the sidewalk as he walked directly in front of Pip's car.

"Good Lord," murmured Pip. He turned his head and watched aghast as Kilroy walked a few yards then stooped to tie one of his plaid shoelaces. In the red platform shoes Kilroy must have been almost six feet tall. Six feet of pure, freaked out punk. "I'm counting ways he violates St. Bartolf's dress code," Pip whispered in Sam's ear, "and I've already gotten to twenty-six."

"Shhh," said Sam. "He might hear you."

"What is he? Some mean green mother from outer space?"

"Another new staff member on the *Traveler*," Sam explained.

"Don't worry about me," said Luke blandly. "You two just make yourself comfortable."

Sam looked up to see Luke leaning on the hood of the car.

"You could sit in his lap, Sam," Luke suggested kindly. "I can't help but notice that you're a little cramped for space there with Pip's knee up against the gearshift and your ear pressed against the lock button."

Pip laughed and squirmed back into his own seat. "I thought this parking lot was almost empty. Turns out it's Grand Central Station," he said. He rested his arm on top of the steering wheel and regarded Luke with amused tolerance.

"You were great in there, Luke," Sam said. "I was very impressed."

"I think most of them are going to take me up on it," Luke said. "It'll mean some changes in the paper, but changes are what we need, right? This may be the kind of shaking up that'll give the paper a new lease on life." He gazed off into the distance. "It'll be kind of a shock to Happy, though. It's one thing to be Lady Bountiful to the peons, and it's another thing to find yourself on an equal footing with them day after day."

"That's true," said Sam, gulping. The idea of being chummy with the staff of the *Cock and Bull* day after day was one that set her heart palpitating, though she would never have been able to bring herself to admit it.

"But we aren't snobs like that, are we, Sam?" said Luke, merrily slapping the car.

"No, indeed," said Sam faintly.

"Easy on the paint job, Luke," warned Pip.

"Sure." Luke grinned and removed his hand from the hood. "I've got big plans, Sam. One thing in particular I've got in mind for you. Top secret. I'll have to talk to you about it later. I sure wouldn't want to interrupt anything. Well, see you around."

He sauntered off in the direction of his car, the sun making a halo of his hair, his step jaunty.

"I wonder what he means by big plans for you," Pip said, frowning.

"Probably just something about the paper. That's all Luke really thinks about these days is the paper." Sam watched him walk away and leaned closer to Pip. "I didn't like to mention this before, Pip, but lately I have gotten really worried about Luke. I mean, for a minute there he had me thinking he was going to end up in prison."

"Don't give up on that," said Pip. "He might make it yet."

"No, really," she said. "I was really worried. But now I think it's going to be all right. Do you see how he's pulled himself together?"

Pip cast a pointed look at Luke as he got to his car, his ragged shirttail flapping in the breeze, a jagged tear in the leg of his pants visible at fifty paces.

"Emotionally, I mean," Sam clarified hastily. "He's really got it together. He knows what he wants, and he's willing to play by the rules to get it."

As Luke drove off, he honked his horn three times and waved at them.

Sam looked at Pip, puzzled. "Did you ever say why you were waiting for me?"

"Oh, that," said Pip, running his hand over her hair. "I just started thinking about what I said at lunchtime, and I got to feeling like I'd been kind of a jerk. I just thought I shouldn't have said, 'it's him or me.' That's sort of a jerky thing to say."

"That was okay," said Sam blithely. "I didn't pay any attention to it, anyway."

"That's good. I guess. I mean, if he really is just a friend, I suppose I must have sounded stupidly possessive and jealous."

"That's okay, stoopid," said Sam, pecking him on the cheek. "So you're over that now?"

"Yeah," said Pip. He grinned ruefully. "I guess I have to figure that after all, you're kissing me, not him."

"Pip, you don't think that this, well, this attraction that we seem to have to each other is just physical, do you?"

"Who cares?" said Pip, stroking her hair.

"But—"

"I mean, no, Sam! I think we have a lot in common and relate to each other on a profound spiritual and intellectual level. Not to mention that I have a deep respect for you."

"That's good," said Sam, snuggling up against him.

"I just wish the heck I knew what Luke had up his sleeve," he said. He lifted his head and seemed to be listening for the roar of the green Pontiac as it tooled merrily away down Thirteenth Street.

* * * * *

Find out what Luke has in mind for Sam.
Watch for the next book in this exciting new
series, The In Crowd.
Coming soon from Keepsake.

Blushing Beauty—Do's and Don'ts

Avoid colors that are very different from your natural cheek color.

A defined line looks unnatural. Blend your rouge well so no one can see where color begins or ends.

Don't blush in a strip so wide that it covers your entire face. Blush is used to highlight cheekbones and add color to the face. Don't overdo.

Never apply blusher too close to the center of your face. Feel your face. Notice that the prominent part of your cheekbone starts around the area under the center of your eye, not at the bridge of your nose.

Practice with gels. A little squirt goes a long way.

Applying blush without a mirror is a mistake. Always watch what you're doing.

Don't apply blush before foundation. If you're wearing foundation, apply it first, blush second.

If you've tried applying a little blush as directed above but feel that you'd like to make a little more (or less) of your face shape, there are a few contouring tricks you can try with cheek color. Be sure to play and practice at home to see what works best for you. A few afternoons in front of the mirror will make you a makeup pro!

1. Think about the shape of your face. Is it square? Round? Rectangular? Triangular? Oval?

2. A hint for the round face: Put a dot of color on your chin and blend it in. This will help lengthen your face a bit.

3. Is your face long and narrow, like a rectangle? To soften the hard lines and widen your face, concentrate blush on the outer edges of your face. This will draw attention away from the length and give more width where you need it.

4. To minimize the hard lines of a square face, apply blusher normally, then dot a bit of extra color on your chin and the middle of your forehead. Blend well.

5. Triangular or heart-shaped face? Avoid putting blusher on your chin. It will only call attention to it.

6. Oval face? Anything goes. Try a hint of blush on earlobes, too, to give a fresh, country look—as if you've just come in from the great outdoors.

COMING NEXT MONTH
FROM
Keepsake

KEEPSAKE # 33
A DARK HORSE
by Emily Hallin

When her dad runs for Congress, Wendy finds herself a winner.

KEEPSAKE # 34
DEAR DR. HEARTBREAK
by Janice Harrell
#2 of The In Crowd *series*

Samantha thought that taking on the role of the mysterious Dr. Heartbreak would be a breeze. Who could be better qualified to dish out advice to the lovelorn?

AVAILABLE NOW

KEEPSAKE # 31
FOREIGN EXCHANGE
Brenda Cole

KEEPSAKE # 32
THE GANG'S ALL HERE
#1 of The In Crowd *series*
Janice Harrell